Penguin Book C 2420

The Telemann Touch

William Haggard is the pseudonym of a writer who was educated at Lancing and Christ Church, Oxford. Entering the Indian Civil Service in 1931 he became a magistrate and sessions judge before joining the Indian Army for service during the Second World War. He passed through the Staff College at Quetta and was promoted to G.S.O.1 on intelligence work. In 1945 he returned to work in Whitehall, where – to quote his own words – 'I've been a layabout ever since'.

William Haggard has travelled widely in the East and South America but prefers now to stick to Europe 'while it lasts'. His other books include *The Arena*, *The Unquiet Sleep*, *Venetian Blind*, the award-winning *The High Wire* (all available as Penguins), *The Antagonists*, *The Powder Barrel* and *The Hard Sell*. They have been translated into most European languages. Living in 'doctor-land', near Harley Street in London, he also maintains a long-standing connexion with Italy, where he has a *pied-à-terre* near Venice.

The Telemann Touch

William Haggard

Penguin Books

Penguin Books Ltd, Harmondsworth,
Middlesex, England
Penguin Books Pty Ltd, Ringwood,
Victoria, Australia

First published by Cassell 1958
Published in Penguin Books 1966

Made and printed in Great Britain by
Hunt Barnard & Co. Ltd, Aylesbury
Set in Monotype Times

For Margaret Russell

Chapter One

In the only slightly cooling evening David Carr was walking back to his bungalow on St Cree's. The island lay a day's journey by launch from the coast of the Colony which in name administered it. At its longest it was perhaps a dozen miles, and only a good map showed it. He was walking with Carey, the head of Universal in the Colony. 'Seventy thousand barrels a day,' Carey was saying; he had been saying it for some time. 'It's incredible.'

'Yes,' David said.

His father, old Jonathan Carr, wouldn't have been astonished that the elder of his sons was a Minister of the Crown, nor that the younger, in the profession he had chosen, had already made something of a mark; but he would have been a little surprised that David had taken to oil. For David had been the bookish one. Old Jonathan had had the Scot's respect for learning, learning above, but not insanely above, material success; and when the learning promised to be materially successful, when the boy had every chance of his Fellowship, Jonathan Carr had been content.

He had sat upon something a little over the four hundred acres of excellent Lowland land. He was the fourth generation of Carrs to work it, and by now it was his own. He was solid, progressive, a man to be accounted. A hundred miles to the south he would have been something more than a notably prosperous farmer; he would have had pretensions.

He had died quite soon after war had swept David from his

second year of research, before he had been decorated. That would have pleased him. He would have accepted it, have known better than to ask questions. But he might have asked questions about Universal, and David was happy that he did not have to answer them, for he could not always answer himself. All that he was sure of was that, when the fighting was over, a Senior Common Room had seemed unthinkable, a life quite impossible. Not that it hadn't satisfied him at the time; not that an oil company, now, completely replaced it. You couldn't, he had decided, have it both ways. He was fortunate to have discovered in time that there *were* two ways, two David Carrs. It was better to be in oil, happy, absorbed, and satisfied for most of the time, than a don fretting for a world of action which he could only sense. Oil was the most potent drug he knew. Mostly it bit beautifully, but occasionally, tonight for instance. . . .

Tonight he was walking home with Carey. 'I guess it at seventy thousand a day,' Carey said again, 'and God knows what to come.'

'Yes,' David repeated.

'There's everything to do, of course – buildings, decent housing, a proper jetty. It might even be worth a pipeline, a big inch, to the mainland. And that's on a singlewell. That's if we never bring in another.'

'Quite so.'

Carey was elated, but David, tonight, was feeling a little flat; he was thinking, prematurely and he knew it, that it had all been tremendous fun. On St Cree's had been an official bungalow, the one the very junior magistrate stayed in twice yearly when, a little reluctantly, he visited the island from the Colony; a village of sorts shambling about what was called the harbour but was in fact a cove; a collection of Kamblas, feckless and dirty. They squatted interminably, picking their noses; spitting; breaking a noisome wind. Nobody seemed to know quite how they existed.

And of course those extraordinary, those charming scoundrels in the hills.

It had been exciting to land on St Cree's, to live in tents until the bungalows went up. The launches and the two little steamers, the tempo of their journeys accelerating, had thrashed to and fro. The amazing mess of equipment had accumulated. Quite soon the crazy efficiency of an exploration party had been in full swing.

David had enjoyed all this and had expected to. This he had asked of oil, and this, mostly, it gave him. The geophysicists had been amusing; they had spoken a language of their own. And after them had come the rig crews, the drillers, hillmen from the Colony, tough, clannish, proud of their craft and despising all others. David had always been happy on a rig. And now there would be Development. Which was exciting, almost intolerably exciting, while it lasted. But in a year or two . . . David shrugged. In a year or two St Cree's would be just another oilfield – a big one, it seemed, perhaps very big indeed. There would be acres of housing, roads and an office block; a commissariat, a cinema, at least two clubs. The magic would have stolen away. David glanced sideways at Carey.

But Carey was off again. 'Seventy thousand a day,' he said for the third time. He seemed to feel that his litany required some variation. 'Pretty heavy, I should think. At least three and a half million tons a year. And from a single well. What's still to come nobody can guess. It's – it's positively Persian.'

'Yes,' David said once more. There didn't seem anything else to say.

'You don't sound very excited. It's a wonderful chance for you, you know. They'll leave you here, I think.' Carey hesitated, his manner becoming at once patronizing and a little insecure. 'They will,' he added, 'if I have any say in it.'

'Thank you very much.'

David, veiling his inspection, looked at Carey again. He

was a big man in his early fifties. He wore a large clipped moustache which bristled above a petulant mouth. The two together gave him an air of slightly spurious masculinity. David thought that he looked like an unkindly caricature of a Rugby Football International in middle life and considerable prosperity. He hid a smile, remembering that that was very nearly what Carey was. He was in middle life, undeniably, and certainly he was prosperous, for to be head of Universal in the Colony was an excellent position excellently paid. But he wasn't quite an International. He had had two trials, two Possibles, but nothing more.

The two men walked to David's bungalow. It was ugly but surprisingly comfortable. Universal was very good at temporary buildings: it had to be. There was a considerable central room, its ceiling supported by triangulated steelwork; but the double roof was of the latest, the most efficient insulator. A veranda, the full length of the northern side, looked upon the beginnings of a garden. Universal thought of everything. There was a bedroom and a bathroom at either end, one a little bigger than the other. David had been sleeping in the bigger, but had moved from it for Carey's visit. Carey took the larger room, the better bathroom, without comment.

A servant brought them what in the circumstances was a very good dinner indeed. Carey ate quickly and rather a lot, but David wasn't particularly hungry. He listened to Carey talk. 'Anything might come of this,' he began again. 'Anything.'

'I suppose it might.'

Carey smiled his carefully bonhomous smile. 'I was saying just now that you didn't seem as excited as I should have thought. I've been thinking about that and I believe I understand. You're afraid of becoming a pedlar, aren't you? You don't want the office work.'

'I don't particularly mind it. Some of it I like.'

Carey smiled again, but David was silent. He was considering the hierarchy of Universal, and its conventions. And not the least of them was that Driller was King. Naturally he was a well-paid King, though nothing compared to a senior executive. But his prestige didn't depend upon his income; it was a matter of mystique: Driller was the tough one, the frontiersman, the man with his shirt off. There was a nostalgia about him. And after Driller the rest of them on the field. The administrator nowhere.

David hid a smile again; he understood the convention, though he was aware that it was a little absurd. The man on the field could produce an ocean of oil – it rather looked as if St Cree's might. And what was the use of an ocean of oil unless you could move it; crack it; sell it? Sell it in one of the oddest markets in the world, half cut-throat, half monopoly.

Yet in Universal 'pedlar' was a term pejorative.

And Carey had returned to it. 'You're being very tactful,' he was saying. 'I appreciate it. I'm an office-wallah myself now.'

'Now', David decided, was rather good. Carey had been a refinery man, a chemical engineer and a very good one. But in the unspoken hierarchy of Universal chemical engineers weren't particularly considered. The Colony had been his first major administrative job. It had been something of a departure to pick him, and to most men it would have been a feather to be flaunted. But it was evident that Carey was a snob.

And he was assuming that David was the same. 'But I wouldn't worry just yet, if I were you,' he said. 'After all it will be years before you're really chairborne. The place will change, of course – it always does. But think of the work – there's mountains still to be done.' His manner changed suddenly. 'You might start on the airstrip,' he suggested briskly.

David shook his head. 'There's not much we can do about

that,' he said, 'unless we move the well.' He was aware that he was being facetious.

But Carey took this seriously. 'You mean drill again?' he asked. 'Deviate it?' He considered this. Drilling was something he knew little about but it flattered him to appear to. 'Hardly,' he said at length. 'The expense would be tremendous, and we couldn't gain more than a few yards.'

'It's going to cost the earth to build another strip.'

'Then it will have to. We can afford it.'

'I imagine so.'

'We've got to have it. That dumbo pilot nearly killed us this morning. And you can't bring people here, not the top brass, in biplanes out of a museum.' Carey yawned. 'Well, that's something to start on, something to keep you out of that chair. I think I shall turn in.'

David went with Carey to his room, seeing that he had everything he needed. He went to his own room and stripped; he brushed his teeth. His image regarded him reflectively from the mirror above the basin. It wasn't a bad face, he thought: the features were good if a little rugged, and the hair climbed from his forehead in a firm line. In a few years, when the beginnings of grey above his ears had thickened, he would grow it a little longer, brushing it back at the sides. It would be decidedly distinguished, like – like the don he wasn't, he remembered a little wryly. There was that scar, of course: it wasn't positively disfiguring, but David was a little ashamed of it, for it had been the result of carelessness. It had been a bayonet fight, before he had been commissioned. A bayonet fight. . . . Short point, long point, short point. Two competent men-at-arms could go on for ten minutes. David had become impatient. He had risked an overpoint, and the other man had caught him on the cheek; laid it open to the bone. The other man . . .

David frowned. That would be seventeen or eighteen years ago – he hadn't been much more than a boy. But still, sometimes, he remembered the other man's face. It would have been comical if it hadn't been terrified. This, he seemed to be saying, what David was doing to him – it simply wasn't fair: it wasn't in the rules. These Unarmed Combat courses . . .

David Carr shrugged irritably. He walked under the shower, adjusting it carefully. The bungalow was very well fitted: the water could be regulated from hot to almost icy cold. David finally got it as he fancied. He did not want a hot shower, and he knew that one too cold would, in five minutes, make him sweat again. He washed in the lukewarm water and dried himself thoroughly. He put on the trousers of his pyjamas. He wound a piece of silk three times round his stomach, for the fan was directly above the bed. He wanted to keep cool but he did not want a chill.

David Carr climbed on to the bed. In the other bedroom Carey was snoring abominably. It did not worry David. He had slept through worse than Carey snoring.

*

If old Jonathan Carr would have been a little puzzled to find his younger son in oil he would in no way have been surprised that his elder was Her Majesty's Secretary of State for the Colonies. For Edward Carr had always been ambitious. Old Jonathan had seen him as a senior civil servant or perhaps in the boardroom of a reasonably important company; but in the respectable genealogy of the Carrs was a Douglas, and Edward Carr had been prepared to take a chance. Politics had been what had attracted him, and he had fought his way stolidly upwards. And it had been a fight, every inch of it. His father would not have allowed his elder son his younger's intelligence, but he would have conceded him character. He had needed it. He had survived the drudgery of the conscientious back-bencher, the years as a Junior Minister miserably underpaid. It had been a struggle, for he wasn't a rich man or even comfortably-to-do. There had been a little journalism, not strikingly successful, a little money picked up on the Market. Edward Carr had never married. He had wanted above all things to reach the Cabinet. That had been his objective, money no more than a means to an end. Now he had achieved it.

He wasn't a brilliant man, or not in the sense in which the word was used by people whom he mostly distrusted. He was conscious that he was regarded as a little old-fashioned: certainly it wouldn't have embarrassed him to be called patriotic. He was a very good Minister.

He was eleven years older than David, and now he sat in the Minister's room. His desk was superbly uncluttered, for he was doing what he considered he was paid to do. He was thinking. He was thinking about St Cree's and about the Colony.

His permanent officials had told him that the situation was extremely complex – they always did, he reflected – but to Edward Carr who had the art of the essential it seemed quite simple. St Cree's was British territory, and so had been since a foreign princess had brought it to the Crown as dowry. With the Colony itself, of course. A British official from the Colony visited it twice yearly; he flew, when he remembered to, the Union Jack. It was true that Laramonda, the Colony's next neighbour along the coast, had always claimed it. It had protested at intervals which by now had almost become agreed. It had protested and its protests had been ignored. For Laramonda, though considerably bigger than the Colony, potentially much richer and more powerful, had been a Comic Republic. Had been – but now wasn't. Laramonda, now, was a dictatorship, Clementi an uncomfortably efficient dictator. Clementi had an army, quite a good army by any standards and, by the standards of his neighbours, a menacingly good one. And Clementi had a doctrine. With the doctrine went an ally. But an ally, Edward Carr reflected.

Laramonda was very inconveniently situated upon the map, Her Majesty's Government by no means the only Power worried about Clementi and his ally.

So that Clementi's protests, Clementi's claims, couldn't be treated quite as were the claims of some ridiculous President; they had become something more than a diplomatic formality, something more than a joke. There had been talk of international litigation, and Edward Carr was aware that he had colleagues who favoured it. He didn't himself; he was prepared to play it long. It was his private opinion that international litigation was a farce.

But seventy thousand barrels a day wasn't a farce at all. It was oil. Oil. . . . The devil of a lot of it already, and no one could guess what to come.

Edward Carr, who believed in taking one step at a time, in eliminating any uncertainty which could be eliminated, had sent for his Legal Adviser and was now awaiting him. He came in quietly. To call on his Minister he wore his best black coat and sponge-bag trousers. His head looked like a Roman emperor's upon a coin considerably rubbed, a little blurred about the edges. He was a competent academic lawyer but could not have earned a shilling at any Bar in the kingdom. That, in a year or two, wouldn't prevent his being knighted.

'Please sit down,' Edward Carr said briefly. 'Now what about St Cree's? Who owns it?'

The Legal Adviser looked a little pained. So bald a question distressed him, offended his sense of the delicacies. 'It's hardly as simple as that, Mr Secretary,' he said. He had never got further with Edward Carr than 'Mr Secretary'.

'I must respectfully dissent. It is perfectly simple, or at bottom it should be. Is it ours or theirs?'

Edward Carr didn't much care for his Legal Adviser, and when he wished he could be very firm. He was in no way ashamed of it.

'The story goes back into the seventeenth century. The Princess . . .'

'I know – I've read a little about it. The State Treaty and the marriage settlement. The variation in the domestic courts. The Treaty d'Albiac, which may or may not have covered Laramonda, which was then a territory of the Power with which we were treating. The Boundaries Commission in the eighties. And all the rest of it. Where does it take us?'

'It takes us into very deep water, I'm afraid.'

'Of course. But do we sink in it or swim?'

The Legal Adviser considered that he was being rushed; he continued to temporize. 'You mustn't think,' he said, 'that on a matter of this importance I should feel able to speak from my own opinion alone. We have had to consult with the Adviser to the Foreign Officer. And we have been to Counsel – very eminent Counsel.'

Edward Carr decided that he had made a mistake. It was one of the reasons for his success as a politician that he could recognize his mistakes very quickly. He decided to change his approach. 'I should have been perfectly satisfied with your own view,' he said smoothly.

'Thank you. That is very kind.' The Legal Adviser stroked his debased imperial nose. 'The best opinion,' he said, 'is inconclusive.'

Edward Carr suppressed a sigh, and something of his original manner returned to him. 'Then let us put it as a bet,' he said. 'As a gamble.'

'As a gamble, Mr Secretary?'

'Why not? Lay me the odds.'

The Legal Adviser was silent; he was thinking that his Minister was a barbarian.

But Edward Carr was looking at his watch. 'Yes,' he was saying, 'the odds. Evens, would you say? Or better? Or are they worse?'

The Adviser still did not answer directly. 'So much,' he

said, 'would depend upon the composition of the Court.' He permitted himself a smile. 'It might even depend upon their livers.'

Edward Carr, but not immediately, recognized a joke. He didn't think it a very good one, but he returned the smile politely. 'Then let us include the composition of the Court and the learned judges' livers along with the other uncertainties. Let us include them in the odds. I am still asking you to lay them.'

The Legal Adviser hesitated. Finally, but with an evident reluctance, he said: 'A little worse than evens.'

'Indeed? Seven to four, would you say? As bad as that?'

The Adviser did some mental arithmetic, for he wasn't a betting man. 'About that, I should think.' He was pricked by a moment of rebellion. 'But you must remember, Mr Secretary,' he added, 'that I am not a member of the Victoria Club.'

'And nor am I. But then, I'm not a bookmaker. I sometimes wish I had been, but I doubt if I could have thought fast enough to make a success of it. I've been taken there, though. Very comfortable club indeed.'

'Is it?' the Adviser inquired a little weakly. He didn't quite know what answer he had expected of his Minister, but he hadn't expected that. He was a timorous man, and his knighthood had still to come through. It should be safe enough by now, but . . .

'You mustn't think, Mr Secretary,' he began.

But Edward Carr was on his feet, walking to the door. 'Not at all,' he said. 'I am greatly obliged to you. To all of you.' He shook hands pleasantly. Incredibly, a little incredulous, the Legal Adviser was in the corridor.

Edward Carr returned to his desk. He began to laugh. The sound of it wasn't cynical, or even superior. He was genuinely amused.

He lit a cigarette, waiting for his next caller. It would be

Lord Brasted – Brasted who, not too long ago, had been plain James Robertson. Edward Carr was conscious that he wasn't in Lord Brasted's class, though he had liked him for a very long time. Lord Brasted was something exceptional, something very different from a persevering and conscientious Minister. Brasted had panache, but he was a man you could do business with. The Minister smiled affectionately. He was expecting a different kind of interview with the Chairman of Universal, and he wasn't disappointed.

His private secretary knocked, and Brasted, all seventeen stone of him, walked in. Against the spareness of Edward Carr he looked enormous, but for a man of his bulk he moved extraordinarily easily. He had thick grey hair, cut *en brosse*, and an eyeglass. It wasn't an affectation. In his young manhood he had damaged an eye and, not fancying glasses, for he had been something of a dandy, had taken to a monocle. Always they had been specially made, and now they were a part of him. Lord Brasted put in his eyeglass when he got up; removed it sometimes after luncheon to clean it; and took it out finally when he went to bed. Which was usually extremely late. He never dropped it, he never played with it. It was the most innocent eyeglass in the land.

Eyeglass apart, Lord Brasted wasn't innocent at all.

'Good morning, Edward,' he began.

'Good morning, James.'

Lord Brasted lit a cheroot. It was a long, thin cheroot, almost black; it was his trademark; it was whispered that it would drop a swarm of bees in half a dozen puffs. Lord Brasted, who was a considerate man, blew the smoke carefully away from the Secretary of State for the Colonies. 'Well?' he inquired.

Edward Carr did not answer at once, for he was thinking that Brasted's appearance was deceptive. And, moreover, that he was aware of it. A great many men had looked at Lord Brasted, at the eyeglass, the cheroots, and the expansive manner. They had looked and they had drawn the too obvious conclusions.

Always it had cost them money.

'Well?' Brasted repeated.

'Not so well. The lawyers have just told me that our title to St Cree's isn't impregnable.'

'Impregnable to whom?'

Edward Carr shrugged. 'To other lawyers, I imagine.'

'Precisely. But lawyers don't yet rule the world, or not quite all of it. It is as well, perhaps.' Lord Brasted pulled again at his cheroot, still blowing the smoke away from Edward Carr. 'I didn't come to talk about the law,' he went on. 'The sort of law we're involved in – no, that *you're* involved in – is law at the highest level. I use the phrase without attempting to define it. But it's very high. So high it vanishes.' Lord Brasted blew a pungent cloud at the ceiling. 'Like that,' he said, watching the smoke lose itself. 'International law . . .'

'Quite so.'

'It is your worry, if I may say so. I am a business man concerned with business. Specifically, the oil business. And since I do not wish to sound disingenuous, sometimes with politics. The politics of oil. But not with public international law. . . . You are with me, I trust?'

Edward Carr nodded.

'Then we can talk comfortably. You want this oil, I imagine?'

'Most certainly we do.'

'Then we shall go ahead with developing St Cree's. Reserving to ourselves,' Lord Brasted went on composedly, 'the right to make your life a misery if you let us down politically.'

Edward Carr smiled. 'I understand,' he said. 'Perfectly.'

Lord Brasted blew another blast at the ceiling. 'Excellent.' He tilted his chair upright again, putting down his cheroot.

'Do you mind if we change the subject?' he asked. 'Do you mind if we talk about your brother?'

'Of course not.'

'He's one of my coming men. I shouldn't want to lose him.'

'Why should you?'

'That's what I'm asking you.'

Edward Carr smiled again. 'You had better explain,' he suggested.

But Brasted did not answer directly. 'The head of my company in the Colony,' he said, 'is a man called Carey. He isn't particularly intelligent, but he's served us well, and oil, in the Colony proper, is something established, something which has just about reached its limit. But your brother I sent to St Cree's.'

'I feel confident he will satisfy you.'

'So do I. But I wasn't thinking of leaving him there for ever.' Lord Brasted went off again at an apparent tangent. 'Oil is a funny business,' he said reflectively. 'Technicians are technicians, and David has seen a good deal of that. Very creditably. And office men are office men. But there is something else and you can't produce it – not by the most careful training. You can't buy it either, for if one thing is certain it is that if you're offered it in terms it will be false.' Lord Brasted picked up his cheroot: it had gone out but unhesitatingly he relit it. 'If I brought him home,' he asked, 'to a job, a really big one, would he jump at it? Or would he leave us?'

Edward Carr was surprised but concealed it, for he wasn't quite sure where this was leading. 'Why should he leave you?' he inquired. He was feeling his way.

'I thought you might know,' Lord Brasted said simply. 'I thought you might tell me.'

Edward Carr considered this. 'I'd tell you, James,' he said, 'if I knew.'

Lord Brasted sighed, and when he spoke again it was as much to himself as to Carr. 'There was a war,' he said. 'It was a decade ago and more. Your brother isn't a boy. But there was a war. . . . And before that there was a College, a very distinguished one, a Lecturer, a Professor perhaps. . . .'

'You are giving me a glimmering.'

'I cannot give you more. I'm putting it very poorly. I'm a fair judge of men, I think – I couldn't have become Chairman unless I had been. But I don't understand them – I've learned enough not to pretend to. But sometimes I sense things. . . .' Lord Brasted sat up sharply; he became again Chairman of Universal. 'I'm talking rubbish,' he said crisply. 'I'm talking like the sort of novel I detest. But there is one reasonable question I can ask you. David is a bachelor – I should like to see him married. Candidly, to anchor him would suit my purpose. He hasn't a girl, I suppose?'

'Damn it, James. . . .'

Lord Brasted held up his hand. 'Answer,' he said, 'or decline to. I shall understand either.'

Edward Carr reflected, deciding that between old friends the question was a proper one. 'The answer,' he said finally, 'is yes and no. You need not tell me that it is unsatisfactory.'

'Meaning one of those understandings which isn't an understanding?'

'I suppose so.'

Lord Brasted made a very surprising gesture. 'Not like that?' he inquired.

The Secretary of State laughed. 'Not like that,' he said, 'at all.'

Lord Brasted rose. 'A pity,' he said. 'A very great pity. Thank you for bearing with an old woman. *Au revoir*.'

*

Sir Francis Eeles was Governor of the Colony and also Commander-in-Chief, which meant that, if and when he had to, he could give orders to a major and two companies of British troops of a battalion which had been on foreign service a little too long. He was a man who worried easily, and tonight he was very worried indeed. He was pacing the drawing-room of Government House, and ordinarily he would have been at ease, for he was very pleased with what he had done with it. The immense room ran the length of the building, an arcaded veranda beyond it. Elegant, faintly feminine Corinthian pilasters broke the walls. Sir Francis had been delighted with them. He had cleared from the room the comfortable Edwardian jumble of his predecessor and had attacked it with a taste for which there was but one, the inevitable word. Now Persian rugs, carefully spaced, lay on the polished floor. There was a grand piano uncluttered by photographs; French furniture; and cannas in tall white vases.

It was a surprising room for a bachelor, and normally it soothed Sir Francis completely. But tonight he was beyond soothing; he was thinking that the Government which employed him were savages; they could be relied upon to blunder; they would blunder into telling him to send troops to St Cree's; blunder into war, war with Clementi, war with...

Sir Francis shivered. He was a sensitive man with a precise, a delicate mind. It would have astonished him to be told that his Minister thought him a clever fool.

Sir Francis began to consider Clementi. He considered him with confidence, for he was certain that he understood him. Clementi's mind would work as did his own, subtly but with accuracy. Clementi wouldn't do anything obvious; he would choose the best weapon, whatever his adversary was least equipped to meet. He would go on protesting about St Cree's, urging arbitration, looking smug, looking injured, where those attitudes paid dividends. But he wouldn't leave it at that – not where a major oilfield was concerned. Not Clementi. His real weapon would be subversion. God knew the ground was ripe for it.

The Governor glanced at his watch. It was almost nine and

he had sent for his Chief Secretary. He did not think much of his judgement, but undeniably he had experience.

Henry Masters arrived punctually. The suns of a dozen improbable stations had wizened him, but he was still upright and alert. He accepted a whisky and soda, thinking that it might have been stronger; he knew the Governor's Allowances and suspected that he was economizing on them. Francis Eeles thought little of Henry Masters; he considered him a useful compendium of local knowledge. Henry Masters had for Francis Eeles an unmitigated, a complete contempt. This he concealed, but not from fear.

Sir Francis began without preamble. 'We are in for trouble, I am afraid.'

'It is certainly possible,' Masters said coolly. He had called the Governor 'Your Excellency' once, when first he had arrived from a desk, a very senior desk, in London, and he had decided that he would use the appellation just once more – when he himself, in a month or two, went home on final retirement. Meanwhile he sipped his whisky and soda. It was even thinner than he had supposed.

'It is inevitable,' the Governor said shortly.

'May I ask how you see it?' Masters inquired.

'But surely that is obvious. Those idiots in Universal have been laying up trouble for themselves ever since they came here. Yes, I know about the Kamblas – they aren't exactly attractive material as employees. I know their failings. But to take these hillmen, these Comingi, to take them exclusively, to turn them into what amounts to a private army, almost a new race . . .'

Henry Masters interrupted. 'Petroleros,' he said, almost to himself; he turned to Sir Francis. 'Have you seen the figures?' he asked. 'They're very interesting.'

'The employment figures, you mean? I haven't, but I can guess them: Universal has ten Comingi for every Kambla. And when a Kambla does have a job it's as a menial.'

'I wasn't thinking of that,' Masters said placidly. 'I was thinking of their measurements.'

'What on earth are you getting at?'

'Did you know that the average Comingo male between sixteen and twenty-five is nineteen pounds heavier than his grandfather and two inches taller? That their women are fairer than many Latins?'

'My very dear Masters . . .'

But Henry Masters went on: in his quiet way he was enjoying himself. 'And that in the hills,' he said, mildly lyrical, 'is a little paradise, a paradise supported by the Company's pensions. Talk about Nepal . . .'

'I do not wish to talk about Nepal. Mercenaries are something I cannot bring myself to admire. Queen Victoria is dead.' His Excellency spoke with asperity; he had intended to be crushing but was conscious that he had not crushed.

Henry Masters was unmoved. 'Quite a few people regret it.'

'For myself I look to the future,' Sir Francis said. It sounded decidedly pompous and he was aware of it.

'May I ask what you see in it?'

'But surely that, too, is obvious? There are several million Kamblas in the Colony: they are discontented and resentful. Already Clementi has men at work amongst them. Not very seriously, I admit. Not as yet. But St Cree's he has claims on – I am by no means persuaded that they're absurd – and St Cree's may be a major oilfield. There are Kamblas on St Cree's also, let me remind you.'

'Two or three thousand,' Masters said.

'And Comingi?'

'A few in the hills. An offshoot, a sort of settlement, from the people here.'

'Precisely. But in any case the work on this new field, the well-paid work, will go to Comingi. To petroleros. The Company will import them.'

'Very probably it will.'

'Then can't you see it, man? It's a situation made for Clementi.'

'I can see it all right.'

'Then what would you suggest?'

'Nothing for the moment. If you are right, and I incline to think you may be, the next move is Clementi's.'

'But good heavens, man, think of them at home.'

Henry Masters didn't much fancy being addressed as 'man', but he did not say so; he had other remedies; he could always make His Excellency lose his temper. 'I am thinking of them,' he said.

'Think of the Office – it's capable of anything.'

'Or of nothing.'

'Then what do you suggest?'

'You could send a dispatch, of course.'

'Certainly I could. And I shall. But do you think they would pay any attention to it?'

The question was rhetorical.

'Frankly, none whatever,' Henry Masters said blandly.

Sir Francis Eeles rose. He realized, not for the first time with his Chief Secretary, that he had had rather the worse of it. If Masters hadn't been retiring in six months . . . 'Good night,' he said briefly.

'Good night.'

The uniformed doorkeeper saluted as Henry Masters went down the steps to his car. He was smiling comfortably. Nobody, he was thinking, could match the arrogance of the office intellectual. He turned the phrase round in his mind, for it wasn't quite what he wanted. He was a little surprised when the just, the perfect word arrived. Nobody, he thought now, had quite the arrogance of the intellectual who was afraid. He whistled almost inaudibly. Like Sir Francis he foresaw trouble. Not quite the same trouble, but trouble all right. And plenty of it.

In the splendid, the slightly effeminate drawing-room, Sir Francis Eeles walked to the piano. He began to play the E flat Nocturne. He did it rather well. His left hand wasn't quite perfect, but for an amateur he was very good indeed. The music quietened him; suited him perfectly.

Chapter Two

David Carr had had a busy day. Already, in under a week, the face of St Cree's had changed. Opposite his bungalow, but not too near to it, the beginnings of an office block climbed steadily. Housing had sprung up everywhere, temporary but by no means uncomfortable housing. The men to fill it, Comingi, petroleros, swept in, carefully phased, as it was finished: four or five men to a building, four or five men to complete five or six more buildings. The apparent chaos had been extremely carefully planned. Electricians swarmed on pre-fabricated pylons. A respectable generator was already working. Piping lay in three huge piles, and a bewildering variety of stores. The dust swirled with purpose. In the little harbour the pile-driver thumped rhythmically.

David was responsible for all this, and personally. He rose with the sun and at night was asleep in ten seconds. He had seen this before, but never as its head. The excitement gripped him; urgency was in the air. Now, borne along by it, unprotestingly, content – now wasn't the time to remember again that in a year or two St Cree's would be as dull as a garden suburb. This was a field in the first frenzy of development, something unmatched outside battle, a mixture of the most careful planning and of incredible improvisation. *Carpe diem.* This was oil, this, to David, the most powerful stimulus he knew. This he had asked of oil, and this it could mostly give him.

Now he had it; now he was completely happy.

This evening he had come home a little earlier than usual: there was still an hour or two of daylight and a moon to come. David decided that he had earned a moment of ease. His leisure wasn't so generous that he could afford to waste it, and in any case he had only one man to talk to on St Cree's, only one friend. It was Mr Martin, the doyen of all petroleros, and a headman, an aristocrat in his own right. Mr Martin wasn't his name, of course, but to have called him otherwise would have been an insult. And you had to get it right: not just Mr Martin – that wasn't quite enough; and not MISTER Martin, for that was clumsy, it showed that you were an outsider; but *Mister* Martin like – like, David reflected, the Regimental Sergeant-Major in a respectable regiment . . . Mister-Martin.

It was perfect.

David took a jeep and a light woollen cardigan and drove to the foot of the hills.

A track of sorts climbed them. The jeep could have mastered it, but it would have been a struggle, and the return in moonlight something more than a hazard. David decided on the footpath. He locked the jeep and took his cardigan; he began to climb.

He had walked in the hills of the Colony often, and these, geographically, were the same hills. They rose from the eastern plain of the island quite gently, but on their further side, where the island ended, dropped impressively into the sea. They were nowhere very high – between three and four thousand feet at the extreme – but the change in scenery, in climate, was notable. David walked on, his spirits rising as the temperature fell. He looked behind him at the plain. It was scabrous with a kind of camel's thorn, criss-crossed and torn by gullies which the rains had eroded. On the single level space was the tiny airstrip. The well's rig, so inconveniently close, was down by now, but David, screwing up his eyes, told himself that he could just identify the Christmas

Tree which had replaced it. It was all very well for Carey to talk grandly about a proper airstrip. With Universal's full resources it would take months.

He turned to the hills again. It was greener here with an occasional tree, deodars or their close cousins. Small streams ran casually nowhere in particular, losing themselves finally in the ever-thirsty plain. In the rains they would be torrents. There was moss on the stones and flowering shrubs. David put on his cardigan; he hadn't been cool since last he was here.

He knew the path perfectly, but its ending never failed him. He was in trees now, between cliffs almost sheer. In the trees it was very nearly dark. He walked deliberately, savouring the final moment. And suddenly it was before him, the Valley, perhaps a mile long and half as much across. It was cupped in the last of the hills, their brows crowned by crumbling stone forts. The Comingi had built them; when, how many generations ago, nobody was certain. They were deserted now, the home of wild black bees. You could lose your life by an indiscretion.

David stopped dead as he always did; he was smiling broadly. He was thinking that it was almost too good to be real; it was the backdrop to some rustic opera. The grass was absurdly green, and comfortable cattle browsed it. The little houses, perhaps a dozen of them, were bright with new paint. David knew that each of them owned a man working for the Company or eating its pension. The Valley was apart, a little nostalgic even, but evidently it wasn't in decay. There was money here, enough of it – the Company's wages sent regularly home or its pensions deservedly enjoyed. And something else. David began to smile again. Later he would inquire about that from Mr Martin. Mr Martin and David were long acquainted. The proper formalities over, the decencies observed, Mr Martin would talk about that.

David began to walk towards a house a little bigger than

the others. It was Mr Martin's. A girl came out to meet him. David hadn't seen her before. She wore a cotton skirt which had come from the Company's store, and above it a black jersey which it was very evident had not. She was a splendid creature, tall, wide-bosomed. A broad red belt joined skirt and jersey. David guessed that it was French. Her toes peeped from her sandals. They were innocent of cosmetic, but they were enchanting toes, and beautifully kept. Even for a Cominga, a Cominga of the blood, her skin was extraordinarily fair. David realized that he was staring.

'Good evening,' the girl said. 'Good evening Mr Carr.'

'How did you know my name?'

'Yesterday I walked to the new shop.' It was eight miles there and eight miles back again. The girl spoke quite casually. 'I wished to buy some medicine,' she went on. 'I was a little costive.'

It sounded extremely improbable.

'Oh,' David said. 'I see.'

He didn't see at all.

'There you were pointed out to me.'

'Oh,' David said again.

'Will you not come in? My father will be delighted that you have called.'

Her English was almost perfect. It was a little archaic, David decided, the sort of English Lord Chesterfield might have spoken to his son when he wasn't writing letters to him. He smiled at the thought and he smiled at the lovely girl. Her arms were bare; her neck rose from the jersey with an Attic elegance. Her hair was wound into the nape of her neck, but not too tightly. It was a bun – positively a bun. It was the severest of styles and the most effective. Only a beauty essayed it.

'Will you not come in?' the girl repeated.

David, very curious indeed, went into the house.

Mr Martin rose to meet him. He was a huge man now, bearded and patriarchal; he wasn't young, but he was still immensely powerful. He turned towards the girl. 'My daughter,' he said. 'My daughter Jala.'

David bowed. The girl held out her hand and he took it. He was more curious than ever.

Mr Martin turned again to his daughter. 'My dear,' he said, 'we have forgotten something. Bring us the wine, please.'

Jala made him the ghost of a curtsy. She slipped away.

'I didn't know you had a daughter,' David said. They had dropped into the vernacular. David had taken trouble with it and spoke it excellently.

'That is understandable. She was only thirteen when my wife died. I was too busy to marry again, too busy,' Mr Martin said, smiling, 'to marry again and make a proper job of it. So I sent her to school in England. It was a very good school. And then to Paris for six months.' Mr Martin hesitated. 'It was a risk, of course.'

'It's been a tremendous success. She's charming; she's a beauty.'

'I'm glad you admire her. I shouldn't have liked an ugly daughter.'

'You haven't got one.'

'Her mother was lovely. I adored her. That,' Mr Martin said simply, 'was another reason for not wanting to marry again.'

Jala returned with a pitcher and three glasses. She poured the wine. David had drunk it often. It was unassuming and good, a great deal better, he knew, than much which people who fancied their palates made an extravagant fuss about in England. Jala finished her pouring. She passed her left hand once across the row of glasses, from right to left; then her right hand twice from left to right.

Mr Martin smiled again. 'I see you haven't forgotten that.'

'Why should I, Father?'

They picked up the glasses and Mr Martin murmured a toast. David answered him. The Comingi had a great many toasts, one for every occasion. This wasn't the most formal, but nor was it too familiar: it was the toast for an honoured guest but not a stranger. They drank with ceremony, and Jala slipped away again.

David and Mr Martin sat down with the wine. The room was spotless and very comfortable, furnished with exactly the sort of furniture which the Governor had contemptuously ejected from his drawing-room. A wood fire crackled in the grate, for here the evening was cool. Above the grate were two appalling oleographs. Both were of men with beards. One was the hero of the Comingo race, a hero by no means mythical. The other was of His Majesty King Edward the Seventh. Mr Martin very greatly admired His Majesty; he was proud that his father had served him. That had been when the Colony had had a regiment of its own, a regiment of Comingi, before it had been disbanded upon some theory that a one-class regiment wasn't contemporary. Besides, the Kamblas had been jealous. Nobody had understood the principle very well and the Comingi hadn't understood it at all; they had resented it bitterly. Not that Mr Martin hadn't done for himself a great deal better with Universal than ever he could as a soldier. But it hadn't been quite the same thing. Universal wasn't quite the equal of the Crown. Not in the Colony. Not yet.

David returned to Mr Martin's daughter. 'You won't keep her long, I'm afraid,' he said.

'I am ready for that. There is nobody here, of course, but boys and old men. The eligibles are working for the Company. But my people aren't uninterested in women: news of a pretty one spreads quickly. Men will come, I don't doubt, and when she fancies one I can buy him for her.'

Mr Martin wasn't being cynical; he spoke with a decent pride. With the Comingi, dowries were of importance. It gave him satisfaction that his daughter could choose unrestrictedly.

David could hear Jala busy in the kitchen. She was singing in a rich contralto. The song David recognized, and he was a little surprised. The Comingi weren't an inhibited people, but even by their own standards this song was scarcely reticent. It was about a girl who lived with her father, and one day a stranger came to the house, a stranger tall and strong, a man who would know what a pretty woman was for, a potent man, a man to get children. . . .

Jala brought in the dinner. There was vegetable soup, a kind of minestrone, and a chicken. There was rice spiced with the chicken's liver and a sort of bay. It was slender mountain rice, exquisitely cooked, each grain separate. There were sweet potatoes, roasted. Afterwards fresh figs; and the wine again; and strong black coffee. It was a meal for a king. The thin hill air had given David an appetite. He ate ravenously. Jala watched him. She was looking pleased.

Mr Martin saw that his guest had finished and made the ceremonial inquiry. 'You are hungry?' he asked.

David knew the proper answer. 'I am excused from food,' he said. He meant it; he did not feel like eating again for a week.

They rose from the table and Jala went again into the kitchen. She began to sing again, but this time David did not recognize the song. He and Mr Martin sat down with their coffee.

'And how is business?' David inquired. He meant the other business, not oil, upon which this delicious valley thrived. It was gun-running.

'Terrible,' Mr Martin said at once.

'I'm sorry to hear that.'

'Not so sorry as I. I'm losing money.' Mr Martin sounded injured.

David did not entirely believe him, for the picture of Mr Martin losing money wasn't a very probable one. David suspected a certain hyperbole; he waited for Mr Martin to go on.

'It's this upstart Clementi,' he said at length. 'Before he got hold of it Laramonda was our best market – they would take whatever we could give them. But now they get their arms from – well, you know where they get their arms from. We can't compete with an organized programme, nor with Clementi's police. There's still a little business further down the coast, but it doesn't amount to much. It never did, you know. Laramonda was our real market. They don't fight each other any longer, though. Now they've got an army. An army.' Mr Martin was contemptuous.

'A pretty good one,' David said reflectively.

'Nothing,' Mr Martin said, and his tone was final, 'nothing will make a soldier out of a Laramondan.'

'Nothing? Not tanks and proper artillery? And aeroplanes? All the things an honest business man can't handle?'

'Nothing,' Mr Martin repeated.

'I very much hope you're right.'

'It doesn't help me, right or wrong. There's more stuff in this valley than we've ever had before. I'm overstocked. I can't turn it over.'

David suppressed a smile; he glanced at his watch and rose. 'I must be going.'

Mr Martin walked on to the veranda and rang a handbell peremptorily. A boy appeared, grinning. He wore a sheepskin coat, the hide reversed. It had been cured imperfectly and the smell wasn't negligible. But the boy himself was very clean. His head was tied in a white cloth. 'Yes, Uncle?'

he said. Mr Martin wasn't his father's brother: it was an honorific.

'Escort His Honour to the bottom of the hills. Escort him to his motor car.'

'It really isn't necessary. I know the way perfectly. And I've brought a torch.'

'I do not doubt it. But you shall not leave my house unaccompanied.'

David bowed. 'I thank you,' he said. This always happened. He knew the drill perfectly.

'My house is Your Honour's.'

'Myself your servant.'

Jala appeared from the kitchen. 'I think I shall come with you,' she said; she was speaking English again. 'I require the exercise.'

David looked at her, smiling. He thought she was magnificent. She glowed with health and with something more.

She didn't need exercise at all.

*

Edward Carr had read the Governor's Savingram twice already, and now he passed it to Lord Brasted. 'This is a little irregular,' he said. 'At least I ought to have it paraphrased.' He smiled grimly. 'And Eeles would be horrified if he thought I was showing his dispatches to the Chairman of Universal in any form. I'm afraid he's not one of your admirers.'

Lord Brasted said something about Sir Francis Eeles. It wasn't very flattering. He read the longish Savingram carefully. 'It's very well drafted,' he said at length. 'It's very clear.'

'It would be. Francis Eeles wrote beautiful Minutes, admirable Briefs for his Minister. Poor Harry Masters did a spell or two in the Office in the usual way, but he was never remarkable on paper. So Francis Eeles is Governor of the Colony, and Harry Masters, who has the negligible qualification of knowing the country inside out, stays on as Chief Secretary. I don't conceal from you that I should have preferred him as Governor. But Eeles wasn't my appointment; he was my predecessor's.'

'Your predecessor was an ass.'

'We must assume the electorate thought so,' the Minister said dryly.

Lord Brasted took one of his cheroots from an ancient leather case. He did not need to cut the end; he lit it, and Carr's cigarette, casually, from the same match; he read the Savingram again. 'It's partly true,' he admitted. 'What we have done with the Comingi – done *to* them – was a risk. But I should argue that we had no choice. If anybody suggests that we could have extracted oil from the Colony on Kambla labour they are a very long way from reality.' Lord Brasted blew a formidable cloud from his cheroot. 'I am putting it,' he went on, 'at the practical level; I could plead, but will not, that Comingi are very much *nicer* than Kamblas. Extraordinary people,' he added reflectively. 'Nobody knows anything about them really. There's a little Spanish in them by now, and what there is is the purest. Not a drop of Negro, and they aren't Indians. Nobody knows where they came from originally. They're an anthropologist's benefit.'

'And they don't like the Kamblas.'

'They despise them utterly.'

'And the Kamblas are jealous and resentful.'

'I don't doubt it,' Brasted said.

'From which His Excellency deduces a situation dangerous and indeed explosive. I quote.'

'I think he is both right and wrong. It is a situation, certainly, but my Company, which isn't quite so stupid as Eeles imagines, has accepted it. We will even accept that our chickens may one day return to roost. But I deny that the situation is explosive. I think that it can be held for at least a generation. We shall all be dead, perhaps oil will be unimportant, before it breaks.'

The Secretary of State considered this. 'You may be right,' he said, 'and barring outside interference I believe you are. But outside interference is precisely what is making Eeles's flesh creep.'

'He scares very easily, that man.'

'I know he does. He is also a politically minded civil servant, and that's something I mistrust; he has Views – Views with a capital; and he is conscious that Governments don't last for ever. He looks over his shoulder. As I say, I would much rather have had Masters. But right or wrong what he says is sound analysis. I am asking your opinion of it.'

For answer Lord Brasted read from the dispatch. ' "The situation",' he announced, ' "is one ripe for the classic expedients of agitation and infiltration. I cannot persuade myself that Clementi will not take advantage of it." ' Lord Brasted reflected. 'And what do you make of that?'

Edward Carr smiled. 'I was asking you,' he said.

'I think it is a political problem and therefore one for yourself.'

'Come off it, James.'

'But I am entirely serious. I believe there are about a couple of thousand Kamblas on St Cree's, and one or two more we shall probably have to bring in. We shall employ them, I'm afraid, in the positions for which they are fitted. Which are admittedly very lowly. Whilst the Comingi take the skilled, the paying jobs. By that means – you have suggested no other, may I remind you? and nor has Eeles – by that means we hope to obtain for you a very substantial quantity of oil, perhaps before too long a quantity which would tip the balance permanently in your favour. You have told me that you want it, and I would not have believed you if you had said otherwise. In return I am entitled to ask that if any trouble is made for us politically it should be met politically. If anything is done on St Cree's to embarrass us I feel entitled to ask for protection.'

'Protection,' Edward Carr said sharply. It wasn't a word he had heard Lord Brasted use before.

'Protection,' Brasted repeated.

The Secretary of State thought for some time. 'Assuming Eeles were right,' he asked, 'how would you see this developing?'

'I should see agitators working amongst the Kamblas – subversionists. I should see labour withheld, an open strike perhaps. And perhaps, if Clementi is really as dangerous as Eeles supposes, perhaps even violence.'

'You would, eh? Then may I ask how I am to meet it?'

For a moment the slanting sun caught Lord Brasted's monocle. It glinted ironically. 'It is easier to tell you how you can not,' he said; he read from the Savingram again. ' "The classic expedients of agitation and infiltration," ' he repeated; he raised his badger's head from the dispatch. 'And the classic remedies are counter-infiltration, counter-propaganda, counter-espionage. But I imagine you can't use them.'

'I'm afraid you're right. There are Cloak and Dagger people, of course, but St Cree's would be a long way outside their territory. How many men speak Kambla, for instance?'

Lord Brasted did not reply. 'But there are troops in the Colony,' he said mildly.

'Whom I certainly couldn't use.'

'Why not?'

'One reason you can guess: the Cabinet, as it stands, would never let me. You know the political balance as well as I do. I don't ask you to sympathize about that, so I'll give you a better reason.'

'I should be interested,' Brasted said.

'Then it goes something like this: Clementi has claims against St Cree's – that it's his territory, I mean. They're legal claims, and there has been the usual talk of arbitration and so on. All that I am playing long; I think I have it deadlocked where the deadlock matters. The one thing we don't want to do is to break the deadlock, and the one thing which might break it would be something on our part which could be alleged to be an open illegality. Such, for instance, as putting troops on to St Cree's when there was an agreement with Laramonda in the eighties that neither of us would militarize the off-shore islands. I don't suppose any ordinary man is going to believe that putting a couple of companies onto an island is militarization, but it's just the sort of point Clementi can be relied upon to run. It's a lawyer's point too, and we're dealing with lawyers. It would open the door to discussion of what we particularly don't want discussed.'

'I see,' Lord Brasted said simply. 'I didn't know that. Thank you for telling me.' He appeared to come to a decision. 'I will try to return the compliment. How good is your Intelligence?'

The Secretary of State smiled. 'Not brilliant, I dare say, but better than some people suppose.'

'Then did you know that a man called Telemann was in Laramonda? He seems to have been lent to Clementi.'

Edward Carr whistled. 'I didn't know that,' he admitted.

'We're not sure ourselves, but . . . '

'Telemann is pretty big fish. Telemann is trouble.'

'He's that all right.'

Edward Carr began to consider Telemann, for he had heard a great deal about him. Telemann was something more than an agitator, a subversionist of international class. It didn't particularly distress him that Telemann killed with his own hands; he was inclined to give him credit for that – at least he did his own dirty work. But any cold killing, any killing at orders and for a principle, was repellent. It didn't matter whether the principle was right or wrong – the Minister happened to think it quite mistaken. What shocked him was blind, impersonal killing. Damn it, he thought, the man must be committed, utterly dedicated. And that, to Edward Carr, was revolting. Telemann must be an animal, but an animal which had once had a brain.

The Secretary of State returned to Lord Brasted. 'The suggestion,' he said, 'is that Telemann has been lent to Clementi: that wouldn't have been done for some minor trouble-making. So the inference is that Clementi means business.'

'It looks like it, if we're right. Telemann is something much more than just a gorilla; he's heavy calibre.' Lord Brasted in turn considered. 'What's his nationality,' he asked, 'at the moment?'

The Secretary of State told him.

Lord Brasted looked serious, reflecting again. 'So that you could deport him,' he inquired, 'if he got to St Cree's unauthorizedly?'

'We could – if we could lay hands on him.'

'On an island twelve miles long?'

'And postulating, as Eeles does, several thousand sympathizers?'

'I take your point,' Brasted said briefly.

The two men fell into a silence which Edward Carr finally broke. 'Where have we got to?' he asked.

'Somewhere rather unpleasant, I'm afraid. We seem to be agreeing with Francis Eeles, though for rather different reasons. I don't think he knows about Telemann yet – we haven't told him ourselves, and if he had known independently it's safe to assume he would have mentioned it to you. Just the same we're not sure about Telemann, and if we're wrong I still think the position can be held. Against run-of-the-mill subversion and agitation, I mean. Your brother is the man to hold it. I'm not pretending to have foreseen any of this when I sent him to St Cree's, but now that it's happened I couldn't think of a man more suitable. He speaks Kambla as well as Comingo. I can't believe he likes the brutes – nobody does – but he has understanding as well as brains. The combination is extremely effective.... No, I cannot think of anyone better.'

'Rather a responsibility, isn't it?' Edward Carr suggested. 'He's still quite young.'

'You would like me to withdraw him?' Lord Brasted inquired smoothly.

'Certainly not.' Edward Carr hesitated. 'But James,' he said at length, 'I am entitled to ask that, if you leave him, you leave him also a complete discretion.'

'Of course I shall.' Lord Brasted looked surprised. 'I'm not very sure that I understand you.'

'Your Company has a certain reputation.'

Lord Brasted, now, was amused; his stomach shook gently. 'For strong-arm stuff?' he inquired. 'For a little quiet skull-duggery? Well, I won't insult you by denying it totally. Oil isn't won by the methods of Learned Counsel in Chambers. I'm not going to say that even today an individual who annoyed us might not live to regret it or, if conditions were wild enough, that he might even not live. But the palmy days are over, at least in the Colony. Yes, definitely in the Colony. A little quiet nonsense – well, perhaps. But the operative word is nowadays "quiet". Very quiet. Some of the older hands regret it. We don't break labour troubles by violence, if that's what you're thinking of.' Lord Brasted looked solemn. 'Nothing overt. Nothing to risk a scandal.' His cool blue eyes became mischievous. 'We move with the times,' he added. 'We are ever so progressive. Or you could simply say that we do not dare.'

But Edward Carr wasn't entirely satisfied. 'But you were saying,' he suggested, 'that some of the older hands ...'

'If you're thinking of Carey you can forget it. Carey is where he is by something of an accident, but I don't think he's a fool.' Lord Brasted rose. 'God help you, Edward,' he said.

*

David Carr was pouring himself a whisky and soda when he was aware that he was not alone. He turned round sharply. A man had come on to the veranda and was standing in the doorway to the living-room. 'Good evening,' he said. 'I am sorry to have intruded, but I could not find a servant.'

'Not at all.'

The visitor gave David a stiff little bow. 'They call me Telemann,' he said, 'and I have come to make trouble for you.'

David regarded him with interest, for he too had heard of him. He wasn't very tall, but he was beautifully built. He was wearing a dark suit, though the evening was sweltering. But he did not seem to be sweating. In his hand was a hard black hat: it looked absurdly formal. David could see that he was armed. His head was shaven. His eyes were black, his manners hidalgo, and his English excellent.

David poured another drink and handed it to Telemann. He seemed to hesitate but finally he accepted it. 'Take your coat off,' David suggested. 'I was going on to the veranda.'

They walked to the veranda together, stretching themselves on long chairs. David considered his visitor. 'Why do you tell me this?' he asked.

Telemann did not smile. 'I'm afraid it's bravado,' he said simply. 'It is a weakness.... Bravado then, but something else as well.'

'May I ask what?'

'I wanted to meet you before I killed you. I had heard well of you.'

'Thank you.'

'I had heard that you were intelligent.'

'You're really very kind.'

'It makes no difference, of course. Your Company will be driven from St Cree's. It is inevitable.'

'I thought the word was ineluctable,' David said.

Something happened to Telemann's face which in another man would have been a smile. 'It is,' he admitted, 'but it is a very tiresome one. And did I not say that I heard you were intelligent? There are things which you may do to an intelligent man, things which you often must. But you may not be a bore.'

'I don't think you're a bore,' David said levelly.

Telemann inclined his head and David looked at him again; he was thinking that this was something unusual in subversionists. 'How did you get here?' he asked.

'There is no harm, since I have arrived, in telling you. I was dropped from a seaplane a mile or so from the coast. By night, naturally. I had a rubber dinghy and I paddled it ashore. Then I destroyed it.'

'Why?'

'I thought it unnecessary myself, even a little melodramatic. I could have hidden it, as I can hide myself. But those were my instructions.'

'And you always obey your instructions – even when they are rather silly?'

'Always.'

'Well, you couldn't have returned in it, anyway – not to where I imagine you came from.'

'I came from Laramonda,' Telemann said.

'With instructions to kill me?'

'By no means. You, if I may say so without offence, you personally are incidental. My instructions are to make the working of your Company on this island impossible. And to effect its return to my present master. Who is, of course, its rightful owner,' Telemann added.

It had been an afterthought.

'I see.'

'I do sincerely hope so. I hope you won't stand in the way of what is – is inevitable. What I had heard of you predisposed me to like you, and now that we have met. . . . You are not at all the average oil man, you know.'

'You're extraordinarily arrogant,' David said.

Telemann's expression did not change. 'Not arrogant,' he suggested. 'I'm not very sure the word has meaning.' He thought for a moment. 'You have read what I have? Or some of it?'

David understood him. 'I have,' he said.

'May I ask your opinion of it?'

'As dialectic it's undeniably elegant. It's even persuasive. But I don't accept it.'

'Why not if you find it persuasive?'

David smiled. 'Why should I accept it? I've nothing to gain by it.'

Telemann inclined his head again. 'You couldn't have given a better answer. We understand each other, that is evident. Perfectly. I was rather afraid we might, for it will be with regret that I shall kill you. I shall be obliged to – I can see that. But it will be regretfully. That is another weakness, of course, a personal failing, and I am ashamed of it. But it can make no difference.' Telemann picked up his coat again. It had been lying across the arm of his chair, very close, the pocket with the pistol in it uppermost. He rose. 'Thank you for the whisky,' he said.

'Not at all.'

'Good night, then.'

'Good night.'

Telemann went down the steps of the veranda and David returned to his chair. He wasn't angry. He discovered with surprise that he was a little envious. This was something less than a man, and something more. He hadn't a doubt in the world – not one; he knew what he was for; he knew what he wanted.

Which, David reflected a little sourly, was rather more than he could say for himself.

Chapter Three

There was a telephone on the island now, and this morning it shrilled David from sleep. He woke in irritation, for the previous day had been a hard one and he had promised himself to sleep till seven. That, on St Cree's in turmoil, was rather late. He picked up the receiver by his bedside. 'Carr,' he said resignedly.

'Carey here, Carr. I'm flying over to see you. It's urgent.'

'Very well,' David said. There was nothing else to say. He didn't particularly want to talk to Carey.

He bathed and shaved and walked to the airstrip. The tiny plane, low in the sky, rocking a little, grew larger. It bumped to an uneasy stop, its wing tip not a dozen yards from the Christmas Tree on the well. The pilot slid back the window, grinning at David. 'Dicey,' he announced.

Carey clambered out a little awkwardly. 'Good morning,' he said. He inspected the Christmas Tree with a professional stare which was very nearly convincing, shaking his head solemnly. 'I've never been happy about it,' he explained. 'Nobody quite knows what's under there. I used to worry about the gate. . . . '

'Well, we've got the Tree on now.'

'And now I'm not happy about that valve. I've sent for a bigger one. I'll send you a proper Audco.'

'It might be better,' David agreed.

'I'll say it would be better.' Carey had a weakness for speech not entirely his own. 'You remember Montez?'

David nodded, but Carey wasn't to be deprived of his

story. 'Montez blew quite unexpectedly,' he went on. 'Nobody thought it would go wild, but it did. It went in the night. You could see it for thirty miles. It caught, of course – they nearly always do like that.'

'I saw it.'

Carey was a prosaic man, but for a moment poetry of a sort touched him. His expression became almost ecstatic. 'A wall of flame,' he said, 'a fountain of fire.'

'It was terrifying,' David agreed. He had contrived not to smile.

'So I'll send you the biggest there is. There's none in the Colony, of course, but then there's nothing in the Colony like this.' Cary began to show off a little. 'It's mostly quite tame stuff,' he added. 'Pressures, where we don't have to pump, generally quite moderate, and gas nothing special. What we can't use we burn decently.'

David knew all this and a great deal more, but he did not interrupt.

'But this baby . . . ' Carey shrugged a little theatrically, drawing David aside. 'But I didn't come to talk about the well. Have you heard of a man called Telemann?' Carey's manner was conspiratorial.

'I have.'

'Our information is that he's in Laramonda. It seems that he's been lent to Clementi. For trouble, naturally. And the trouble could be here. If he should come here . . . '

'He's arrived.'

Carey seemed to be fighting some emotion; he appeared to master it. 'How do you know?' he asked finally.

'He called on me last night.'

'Well I'm damned. What did you do?'

'We talked of this and that. I rather took to him in a way. He explained that he had come to make trouble for us.'

'Of course he has. But what did you *do*?'

'I gave him a whisky and soda and he went away. What did

you expect me to do? Perhaps I should mention that he had a pistol on him.'

Carey considered this. 'It's serious,' he said at length. 'These damned Kamblas. . . .'

'They're all right in their way. I think I understand it. I can handle them.'

'Perhaps you can. But can you handle Telemann?'

'The two go together, don't they?' David suggested. 'Without the Kamblas Telemann's potential is a little limited. One man . . .'

'An expert. A very dangerous man.'

'By reputation an expert at agitation. A thug on the side. A killer too, he tells me.'

'He threatened you personally?'

'In a way. Not immediately.'

'And you're happy with all this?'

'Of course I'm not – I'm not happy at all. But I don't see what we can do until he shows his hand.'

'But strikes . . . sabotage. . . .'

'There haven't been any yet.'

Carey thought again for some time; finally he shook his head. 'We cannot risk it,' he said. 'How many do you want?'

'How many what?'

Carey smiled. He wasn't a wicked man, and the smile wasn't exactly wicked; but nor was it pleasant. 'Let us say guards,' he said. 'Strong-arm men.' His teeth met suddenly. 'Goons.'

'I don't want any,' David said promptly.

'But my dear fellow, we can't go on like this.'

'We shan't get anywhere by knocking people about.'

'No?'

'No.'

Carey's manner changed. 'I have a responsibility,' he began.

'If you're telling me that you're the boss . . . '

'I didn't want to put it like that.'

David made no answer, and they walked towards the biplane. Carey hauled himself in. In the doorway he turned to David again. 'You're a funny chap,' he said.

'I'm a realist,' David said smiling. He stepped back as the pilot started his engine. The plane turned on one wheel and began to taxi away. It was all very casual. David could see Carey waving to him, and he waved in return.

I'm a realist, he thought, and perhaps a bit of a fool. But at least I've grown up.

David returned to his bungalow depressed. There were a dozen things to do as St Cree's galloped from an inconsiderable island to an oilfield of perhaps major importance. More men, all Comingi, were arriving that morning, craftsmen and minor technicians: they had to be put into their quarters, to be properly settled in. There were stores arriving too: they had to be accommodated. And in the little harbour there was some difficulty with the jetty.

But David, this morning, was without zest – Carey had stolen it. He sat down in the veranda a little heavily, for he was conscious that his enemy was upon him. He wasn't a man much interested in the anatomy of his intentions, but only that they be fulfilled; he had a word of his own for that sort of thing – psycholowoggy. He saw his problem in the simplest of terms: he, David, was still undecided.

He was surprised to find himself calculating that if he wanted to leave the Company he could do so. He had been paying the maximum into the provident fund from the day he joined and Universal had been dutifully doubling it. He hadn't been extravagant and in addition had saved something privately. This he had entrusted to Edward and, as he had expected, Edward had been clever with it. There must be a respectable sum by now. And finally there was his share of the farm. His brother-in-law managed it, but if he wanted the capital instead of an income he didn't doubt that the others would buy him out. David smiled. They would buy him out very promptly, he decided. The farm was really an excellent investment.

The smile faded again. David wriggled his shoulders, but the other David Carr did not leave them. He did not know what he desired and he was angry with himself. You couldn't, he insisted, have it both ways. The argument was solid, unanswerable. Today it didn't help.

He tried again to free himself, asking what in fact he would do – could do – if he left the Company.... Return to his College? But that was impossible now. Teach in some school or other? He was too old. Write for a Saturday paper? David grimaced. A gentleman of leisure then – a decent but rather limited leisure? He pulled a face again. He didn't want leisure; he didn't want to be a County Councillor.

David sighed. This was absurd, he thought; he was worse than some subaltern with arty leanings, it was stupid....

On an impulse he rose from his chair, walking across to the rising office building. There were two European assistants now, and David found one of them. 'I'm a little off colour,' he said briefly. 'I think I'll take a jeep and go to the Valley. I'll be back this evening, of course. Meet me in the bungalow if there's anything particularly urgent.'

'All right, sir. I hope there won't be.' The assistant was rather pleased to be left in charge.

David took his jeep and drove to the bottom of the hills. He decided to drive on. The jeep rocked and groaned over the terrifying track, bucking him ill-naturedly. In its way it was almost more tiring than walking, but it was much quicker. The track converged on the footpath at the mouth of the Valley and David left the jeep in the little wood. The track ran on across the Valley, losing itself in the final rim of the surrounding hills, but David would never take a vehicle into this lovely place. He wouldn't have minded if he had been called sentimental about it.

He climbed from the hard seat stiffly and walked to Mr Martin's house. He knocked and waited; he knocked again. Jala appeared suddenly. Her brown hair was down her back, free as a mare's mane but longer. She was wearing a dressing gown. David had heard of women sitting on their hair; it was a respectable convention, but the reality, the sight of a woman who could evidently do so, was surprising. He found himself thinking that Jala, sitting on her hair . . .

'Good morning,' Jala said. 'You must overlook me, please. I was washing my hair.'

'Not at all.' David discovered that he was staring again. 'I had hoped to catch your father.'

'Father is hunting. He has gone down the cliffs.'

It was a formula: it meant that Mr Martin was away gun-running. He had gone down the cliffs, three thousand feet of them and more, down the path which the men of this valley knew. At the bottom the sea bit deep into a tremendous cave. In the cave was a schooner, its motor Mr Martin's pride.

Mr Martin was about his business.

'I'm sorry to have missed him,' David said; he held out his hand and Jala took it.

She was in his arms in the same movement. Even without shoes she was almost as tall as he. He could feel her body against him, superbly alive. He pulled her long hair gently and her lovely face rose to him. He was conscious that under the dressing gown she was naked.

He broke from her finally; he was shaken but happy. His enemy had departed. 'I must go,' he said.

Jala looked astonished. 'But why?'

'I must go. Indeed I must.'

'But you cannot. If my father hears that you have been here and that you have gone without food he would beat me.'

David looked at her, hesitating; he decided that she was

telling the bare truth. 'Does he often beat you?' he asked, smiling.

'Never. But he would if I were not hospitable.'

David still hesitated; he had reason to. 'Very well,' he said at last. 'And thank you.'

They went together into the speckless little kitchen. David's spirits had risen absurdly. He was handy in a kitchen and enjoyed cooking; he looked about him with satisfaction.

'What would you like?' Jala inquired. She had slipped into Comingo.

David gave her the proper answer. 'Your crust is my feast,' he said.

'Your presence an ornament.'

They laughed together delightedly.

A huge haunch of bacon hung, opulent, from the ceiling. David pointed to it. 'It looks very appetizing,' he said.

'With eggs then?'

'With eggs, please.'

They moved to the range. David took a frying pan from the shining row of utensils and began to fry the eggs and bacon. At the other end of the stove Jala was busy with pimentos and sweet corn. It wasn't a big stove and they were very close. Jala was against him again, like an enormous cat, he thought, and with a cat's abandon. He took her again and kissed her, not like a cat at all. She was still wearing the dressing gown.

'You're burning the eggs,' she said presently.

They moved to the table and Jala brought coffee and home-baked bread. 'Do you always eat like this?' David asked.

Jala was evidently pleased. 'You like it?'

'I know nowhere I can eat better. Nowhere in the world.'

'Then eat here often. Eat always.'

David laughed. 'I wish I could.'

Jala seemed to take this seriously; she considered for some time. 'Father's very rich,' she said at length. It was spoken quite innocently: she meant that her father could afford to be hospitable. 'He has the pension,' she went on, 'and the – the hunting. And some land too.' She looked at David unexpectedly. 'Do you have land?' she asked.

'A little.'

'That is good. Tell me.'

'I've a third share in what was my father's farm. My brother has another share and my sister the last. Her husband manages it for all of us. But I was thinking of selling it. I was thinking about it this morning as it happens.'

'But why?'

'I can't explain – I don't know myself.'

Jala shook her head. 'Do not sell it,' she said. 'A man should have land – always.' She was speaking very seriously. David thought her enchanting. 'Men go away. They go away, and they have adventures, and sometimes they make fortunes. But always they should have land. A little, even – but something. That is a part of a good man. A good man has land behind him. That is better.' Jala smiled suddenly. 'And a woman is best,' she added.

'The right woman,' David said. He was thinking again that Jala was delightful; he was thinking too that she was very wise.

'But of course.'

David looked from the window, astonished how far the afternoon had faded. 'I must go,' he said once more.

Jala seemed surprised again. 'Why?' she asked simply.

David couldn't think of an answer which didn't sound silly. 'I must go,' he repeated. 'But first I must help you wash up.'

Jala was scandalized. 'Oh no,' she said.

'Oh yes.'

David pushed her before him to the sink. It was true, he decided – she could certainly sit on that hair. He pushed her a little more shrewdly than was strictly necessary. Jala didn't giggle; she accepted it as her due. They washed and dried up in a comfortable silence.

Jala came with David to the door. She was in his arms again, generous, magnificently uncomplicated. He found that he could give her nothing which she could not return him.

He broke from her finally and walked to the jeep. Behind him he could hear her singing. It was that song again. He did not look back.

He climbed into the jeep and began to ease it down the track. If anything it was worse going down, but David drove easily now, relaxed. That is a woman, he was thinking. But a woman. He had never met one like her. Never. She wasn't, for instance, a bit like Margaret Harrison.

He was pleased that no assistant was waiting for him in the bungalow, for he wanted to think. He waved aside with an apology the food which his servant offered him and went to the veranda with a drink. He began to consider the afternoon but he did not get far with it. The noise outside, barely noticeable at first, increased suddenly. There was the sound of men running; shouts; the thud of blows; and something which might have been a groan. David jumped from his chair, taking the steps of the veranda in a single stride, running to the knot of struggling men. Two of them were on the ground, locked obscenely. As one came uppermost the others struck at him. They were striking with skill and knowledge.

Carey, David thought – Carey hasn't wasted any time.

He came to the fighting men; he was furious. 'Stop it,' he said. It hadn't occurred to him that he might not be obeyed: his voice bore a complete authority. The three men standing drew back. They were dressed in the unwholesome rags of Kamblas, but David could see that they were not. He stooped to the two on the ground, still struggling. The one in the clothes of a Kambla came suddenly uppermost. David put one hand beneath his chin and the other, the fingers bunched curiously, into the nape of his neck. The man gave a sudden gasp. 'All right,' he said.

He raised himself slowly, rubbing his neck. David kicked him. He didn't kick to hurt; he kicked in contempt, and appropriately. He looked at the four men. 'Now go to hell,' he said.

For a moment the four men hesitated. Then one of them made a gesture which might almost have been a salute. 'Very good, sir,' he said.

'Then be off. And quickly.'

David did not look at them again. He bent to the man still on the ground. He saw at once that it was Telemann. He was nearly naked, his face a bloody mask, but it was Telemann. David felt him carefully: his pistol had gone. His right arm was doubled under him and David released it. He ran his hand along it. 'Nothing actually broken,' he said, 'as far as I can tell.' He raised himself and looked at Telemann. He was entirely still, only his bright eyes moving. He wasn't groaning. David was conscious that this was a man.

He could have carried him but something, some knowledge of the other, some sympathy deterred him. Telemann wouldn't like to be carried about. Instead David bent to him again. 'Can you use your left arm?'

Telemann nodded.

'Then put it like this.' David knelt down, astride the other and leaning over him. He put his left arm under his own right, across his back. Very gently he pulled Telemann up till he was sitting. He hadn't made a sound.

'Can you get up?'

Telemann put his left hand to the ground, testing the arm; he rolled a little to his left, bracing his right leg. Very slowly he pushed himself to his feet. He swayed and David caught him. 'Take it easy,' he said. 'You need a doctor. I'll take you to the bungalow.'

Telemann's livid lips parted. 'I will not come,' he said through broken teeth. 'I will not be beholden.'

'Don't be a fool, man. I understand you, or I think I do, and you haven't a choice. If I shout you will be taken anyway. I could carry you alone for that matter. You are not beholden.'

David put Telemann's left arm around his neck and very carefully, step by step, they fought their way back to the bungalow. David put Telemann into a chair: he gave him brandy in a tumbler. It was more than half full.

Telemann shook his head. 'No,' he said.

'But it's yes, I'm afraid. Do you want me to call the servants?'

Telemann drank the brandy in two mouthfuls. His breathing became a little easier.

'And no doctor?'

The scarlet mask which had been Telemann's face split for a second. 'No doctor,' it said.

'I understand.'

David inspected his visitor professionally; he had seen rather worse, he decided. Telemann was reviving. David lit a cigarette and put it between the ruined lips. Telemann drew deeply. He smoked the cigarette to the end; he spat out the butt.

'Better?' David asked.

'I must go.'

'Not yet.' Gently but with a firmness beyond misunderstanding David raised Telemann from his chair. He walked him to the bedroom and sat him on the bed. He filled the wash-basin and took from the cupboard the Company's first-aid box. It was an admirable, a comprehensive selection. He took a shirt and a pair of drill trousers from a drawer, putting them on the bed. 'There you are,' he said finally. 'Fix yourself.' He returned to the veranda.

It was a full half-hour before Telemann emerged. David

inspected him once more. He's made a very good job of it, he thought. Telemann was clothed again. His face was a mass of plaster, such skin as was visible brown with some disinfectant. Most of his teeth had gone. He walked with a painful limp and his right arm hung uselessly. David got up and felt it again; he shook his head. 'The hell of a thump,' he said, 'but nothing's gone. The shoulder isn't out, either.' He stepped back for final inspection. Telemann had taken a beating.

Telemann stood hesitant, but David was decisive. He put him into the chair again and brought another brandy. Telemann held out his hand but dropped it again. 'Drink it,' David said sharply. He poured a whisky for himself, slipping into the chair beside his guest. They were silent for some time.

'This is very irregular,' Telemann said at last. He spoke with difficulty through his plastered lips. 'Very irregular indeed.'

'I suppose it is.'

'In my country to accept a drink has a certain significance.'

'Your country is not unique,' David said dryly.

'You are putting me in a position which for a man of honour is intolerable.'

David did not smile. 'I'm sorry,' he said.

'I must insist that your hospitality can make no difference. I cannot have you under any misapprehension.'

'I am not.'

'I may still have to kill you.'

'So you said before. May I again ask why?'

'Because I shall not be able to frighten you away. And you are too good at your job. You understand these Kamblas. You have great influence with them – they tell me so. I judge that you have more influence with them than any other man in your Company. It is probably because you don't try too hard. I think they trust you.'

David was silent and Telemann sighed. 'It is a pity,' he

said. 'I should have liked to know you better; I should have liked to converse with you, to argue.'

'So should I.' David spoke simply. He was remembering that in all the Colony there was no one, really, with whom he could talk. Not, that is, in Telemann's sense of the word. Perhaps with Telemann to talk to, the other part of him, the part that wasn't oil, the enemy. . . .

But Telemann was talking again. 'I can't persuade you, I suppose,' he was saying. 'I cannot induce you simply to leave St Cree's? They could send another man and I could kill him. Not that that would be necessary, I dare say. It's these Kamblas I'm interested in – they are essential to me. And you alone might hold them. You have something *for* them, I think. I know I cannot frighten you away, but I would like to persuade you.'

'No,' David said.

Telemann lit the cigarette which David passed him. He could do it for himself now, left-handed, with difficulty, but David did not interfere. 'That is final?' Telemann asked through the smoke.

'Not quite.'

David turned suddenly to Telemann. 'I suppose that I couldn't persuade *you* to stay? I know the money wouldn't tempt you, but the work can be interesting, and in the evenings we could argue. . . .'

David was conscious that Telemann would have been smiling if he had been able. 'You are offering me employment?' he asked. 'Here – on St Cree's?'

'I am.'

'Professionally I should be insulted, but personally I am flattered. So I regret . . . I very much regret . . . I do indeed. Genuinely. As you say, we could have talked. . . .'

'Then I'm sorry,' David said again.

Telemann rose with an air of finality; he hobbled down the steps of the veranda, turning at the bottom, giving his stiff little bow. 'Thank you for your help,' he said. 'I will try and repay it.'

*

Sir Francis Eeles was having difficulty with his dispatch, for he was trembling. He poured himself a whisky and soda, something considerably stronger than he had offered to Henry Masters. But still he shook, and not entirely in anger. The fools, he thought, the blundering savages. So this was Universal when you scratched its urbane surface, this was an oil company in a difficulty. Animals . . . beasts. . . .

And dangerous beasts. Dangerous to the peace of the Colony; dangerous to the peace of the world; and dangerous to Francis Eeles.

His Excellency put his pen down, forcing himself to think. He decided that his own position was clear. He was a Governor now, as high in the Service as he could get, and after that was nothing else unless . . .

Unless things went the way he wanted them.

They could, he thought: it wasn't a pipe dream. There would be an election in a year or two, perhaps before, and he had contacts, even friends, where it mattered; intelligent men and women, sensitives, people who realized what century they were living in. Not like Edward Carr, not moderately successful investors, not people who hobnobbed with the Chairmen of oil companies, taking their advice, protecting their squalid interests. His Excellency held a severe opinion of his Minister. It had never occurred to him that it was a superficial one, a judgement on a man imagined, a man neatly labelled, not of the man.

He freshened his whisky and soda. Yes, there would be an election before long, a coalition perhaps – men of right feeling. And then Commissions, statutory bodies and creatures, Advisers to this and to that. There should be something for

Francis Eeles all right, perhaps something considerable. Provided . . .

Provided only that Sir Francis Eeles still carried the right aura, still smelt right. It was terrifyingly easy to smell wrong. The Governor was feeling injured. Life, he considered, was treating him very unfairly. He was on the horns and he resented it. Nobody wanted an ex-Colonial Governor whose tenure had been unsuccessful. Nobody. And a Governor who had been successful as Edward Carr might force him to be successful, distastefully, vigorously, a latter-day Pillar of Empire – his friends certainly wouldn't want that. They would drop him flat.

Sir Francis Eeles took his pen again and began to write. He wrote dispatches very easily. The phrases flowed smoothly onto paper, persuasive, reassuring, and totally false.

Chapter Four

Lord Brasted was walking the Secretary of State's room. He padded to and fro on the balls of his feet, enormous but far from clumsy; he was swearing catholically. 'That bloody fool,' he concluded. 'So I was wrong. That bloody fool Carey.'

Edward Carr smiled, though he was some distance from amusement. 'Will you sack him?' he asked.

'I shall not. I cannot afford the loss of face.'

The Minister's eyebrows rose. 'Face . . . ?' he inquired.

'It's a stupid word, I know: I owe you an explanation of it.' Lord Brasted abandoned his prowl and seated himself in the chair beside the desk, reflecting for a while. 'There are three aspects of it,' he said at length. 'The first is the general – the sheer undesirability of sacking a General Manager on the spot, even of moving him in circumstances which inevitably suggest that he has committed a major error. I needn't, I think, expand on that.'

'You need not.'

'I thank you. And the second is the international aspect. In effect we are fighting Clementi for this oil. My representative in the Colony has done something, something which, however stupid, was intended to embarrass Clementi's plans. . . . So I sack or transfer him. Clementi, it is obvious, will draw certain conclusions. They aren't likely to be limited to the action of my Company: at the lowest it will be assumed that Carey wouldn't have been disciplined if you had been anxious that he should not.' Lord Brasted sighed. 'But I would defer to you on that aspect.'

'There is no need to. From my own seat also anything too overt would be disastrous.'

'Then the third aspect is decisive. I find it a little difficult to put it to you with delicacy, so I won't try. It is the question of the relations between your people and mine in the Colony. Ordinarily they get on surprisingly well together considering the economic disparities. Our people, as soon as they get senior enough, are quietly told to minimize in every way possible the fact that they get twice as much money as their civil servant equivalents. What you tell the civil servants I don't know – probably nothing. We sometimes think we notice in them a tendency to over-compensation, to social airs and graces which mostly are quite imaginary; but generally the two communities live harmoniously. Masters, for instance – he belongs to the Club and plays bridge there. He plays extremely well and it might surprise you what he has won over the years. Nobody minds – they even rather like losing a bit to him as long as it isn't too much. And he's very discreet about that. In short he's well thought of. I cannot say the same for Eeles.' Lord Brasted shook his head. 'Carey versus Eeles or any appearance of it I cannot risk.'

Edward Carr nodded. 'Then what do you suggest?'

'What would *you* do in similar circumstances?'

'In politics or the higher civil service it would be easy: the procedure for kicking a man upstairs is established. You leave him the appearance of authority but remove the reality.'

'Precisely. I had thought of something similar for Carey. I had thought that we might send him an Associate. And between ourselves I should probably instruct this Associate privately that it is to Masters he should look rather than to Eeles.'

'I wouldn't object to that just so long as I don't know anything about it.'

'It is understood.'

There was a silence whilst Lord Brasted coped with one of his cheroots. They smoked very fast and there was half an inch of ash upon it before he spoke again. 'In point of fact,' he went on, 'this stupidity of Carey's isn't necessarily fatal. It has accelerated the crisis, I don't doubt, but this isn't the crisis itself. To have brought it nearer may not be a loss.'

Edward Carr weighed this. 'From your point of view – no,' he said finally. 'But from mine it is awkward. I was explaining the other day that on the question of Clementi's legal claims I was determined to play it long. It's the only way to play it. What above all things I don't want is some new factor to break the deadlock. If Clementi does something desperate, then that will be that: we could probably meet it, and at least it would be a simple issue simply understood. Opinion would probably be with us. What we cannot afford is to be manoeuvred into doing anything ambiguous. That is what Clementi is trading on, naturally.' The Minister tapped the top telegram upon a pile on his desk. 'Eeles takes the same line, though I don't doubt for very different reasons. I've had another dispatch from him. I won't show it to you this time if you don't mind, but in effect and allowing for paraphrase he is urging me to do nothing rash. I judge he is fearful that I may lose my Imperialist head.'

Lord Brasted laughed shortly.

'It's no laughing matter, James. If I could act as freely as you can I would take a leaf out of your book and tie some sort of string on Eeles. But he hasn't given me any sort of excuse. I know he's brittle; I suspect him as a man; but he hasn't put a foot wrong. I cannot send him a watch dog formally, nor even instruct him that it would be wise to lean on Masters. A sensible Governor would be doing that in any case, but Eeles isn't sensible. I think he's a doctrinaire.'

'There's a shorter word,' Brasted said.

'It is a curiosity of the times that in dealings with foreigners any British Government is assumed to be usually wrong, and if the foreigners happen to be coloured, then invariably. That is Eeles's attitude, I think – his personal instinct.'

'It's something more than a curiosity; it's a handicap. To all of us.'

'And it deprives me of the advice of the man on the spot. I should welcome that – I have need of it. But it's no use pretending that I trust Eeles's judgement, and I can't call home Masters and go behind his back. Eeles would like a trip home, by the way; he's hinting as much. It would suit him to be absent if anything happened. I don't think he has much appetite for action.'

Lord Brasted puffed reflectively for some time. Finally he said: 'I might be able to help you.'

'You could?'

'I could call back your brother. I wouldn't mind getting the first-hand picture myself, and you could sound him off the record.'

'It's an idea,' Carr said.

'You approve?'

'Most certainly I do. I'm very grateful.'

'Then I will do so at once. A week or ten days should cover it if he travels by air.'

'It's very good of you, James, but . . .'

'But what?'

The Secretary of State spread his hands. 'You were talking the other day,' he said. 'It was all a little oblique, but as I understood it you had certain doubts about David – doubts whether he still felt he had chosen the right job. If you bring him home now, unexpectedly, confront him with the attractions of civilization, with culture, if you will forgive the word . . .'

'I forgive. But I reach for my gun.'

'Well, it's a bit of a risk, isn't it?'

'I should leave that to you,' Lord Brasted said blandly.

'James, stop being Delphic.'

'I apologize. But you were talking about a girl.'

'I wasn't – you dragged it out of me. And you were talking about anchoring. Suppose he got anchored here? He needn't work for you, you know, even married. He has resources which might surprise you.'

Lord Brasted's eyeglass glittered again sardonically. 'You misunderstand me,' he said evenly. 'I don't particularly want him married; I want him in love. The distinction is important. Marriage sometimes steadies a man who isn't steady, but David is as steady as a rock. I'm not a romantic about marriage.'

'I should not imagine it.'

Edward Carr spoke a little tartly. Lord Brasted had had three wives: the first had been plain Mrs Robertson, the second Lady Robertson, and the third, the incumbent of the moment, was the Viscountess Brasted. She was a very charming woman.

But Lord Brasted was in no way put out. 'You are doubtless referring,' he said calmly, 'to my good fortune in having possessed three wives. You may add an attachment or two of a less formal nature if you insist. And you are reminding me, not very penetratingly if I may say so, of anchors. But I wasn't thinking of money; I wasn't thinking of anything quite as crude as the economic millstone. Attractive women have a natural taste for attractive things. As I understand the word they would cease to be attractive if they had not, and I do not deny that I have spent and therefore have had to acquire a great deal of money for that purpose. The point in that context, if there is one, would be only that I haven't regretted a penny of it.' Lord Brasted examined the Minister from his shrewd blue eyes; he knew that he was a bachelor and he felt that he owed him one. 'Women,' he said, 'can make you absurdly happy. You should try them sometime, Edward.'

'You still haven't told me what you're talking about,' the Minister said.

'I do not define, for I cannot. But I know. Your brother and I have much in common. So I want him in love – completely, magnificently. Then the woman will have him but so shall I. He will stay with Universal; he will stay with oil.'

'It's a little obscure,' Edward Carr said dubiously. He had lived in England for a quarter of a century and more, but sometimes the English still defeated him. Lord Brasted in particular.

'Of course it is, my dear fellow. But I know. I am fat and sixty, but I know.'

The Secretary of State considered for some time. 'I don't think he's in love with this girl,' he said at length. 'Not in the sense which I can only guess is yours. It would be an admirable match, most Chairmen would be delighted, but Brasted, it seems ...'

'Brasted, it seems, is an old fool. It is of course entirely possible.'

Edward Carr smiled. 'Well ...' he began.

But Lord Brasted interrupted him. 'Let us say,' he suggested, 'that I should never have made a Minister. Exegesis isn't my forte. But I have contrived to run a tolerably efficient oil company.' He spoke quite impersonally and he picked up his hat. 'I will have David home in forty-eight hours.'

'It is really very considerate.... You're sure you don't mind my consulting him too?'

'Of course not.' Lord Brasted threw the butt of his cheroot into the street. 'I couldn't prevent it anyway,' he said simply.

*

Idly David Carr turned the switch of the wireless set in the corner, and almost at once the room was filled with the clamour of a popular singer. David listened fascinated. It was all there, he told himself – every imaginable sin: the downwards *portamento*, the intrusive Es in June and moon, the *coup de gloppe*. But he did not silence the radio; he began to smile as he listened. By God the man could sing. His breathing wasn't bad; it was evident that he could support a phrase much longer than the slobber he was singing required of him. He broke every rule, but he was aware of every rule he was breaking. David, horrified but unoffended, listened appreciatively. 'He must be making a lot of money,' he said aloud.

He flicked the switch and, surprisingly, he was at Evensong in the Colony's cathedral. Men's voices were throwing a Gregorian confidently across the choir. It was *Tonus Peregrinus*. 'When Israel came out of Egypt and the house of Jacob from among the strange children.' The house of Jacob from among the strange children.... The smile faded. It was stupid to be thinking that in another world were country churches cradled between immemorial farmlands, cloisters and cathedral closes framed in the decencies of Georgian houses. White-painted windows and carved doorcases. Minute walled gardens, suddenly discovered, as secret as a lover. Order and the ancient ways . . .

Outside the bungalow the arc lamps flared in the sweltering dusk.

The telephone rang with a note of urgency. It was Carey again, and he was talking rather quickly. 'Carr,' he began. 'There's an Immediate telegram from the Old Man. You're to fly home at once. For consultation, it seems.'

Carey didn't precisely sound resentful, but it was evident that he wasn't delighted.

'When?' David asked.

'Tomorrow. The plane comes in at nine and will turn straight round with another crew. I'll send the birdcage to pick you up.'

'Thank you very much.'

Carey seemed to be hesitating. At length he said: 'The

Old Man is sending me a – a sort of Number Two, you know.'

David suppressed a whistle. Brasted, he thought – the old fox. 'Who is he?' he asked.

Carey told him.

'I see,' David said. He saw very well. Carey was finished.

'Well, there it is. I thought you'd like to know. . . . The pick-up will be over on the island by nine o'clock.'

'Make it ten.'

'That'll be running it pretty fine, won't it? The big plane is due here not much before, and they aim to refuel and turn around in a couple of hours at the outside. There'll be hell if you miss it.'

'Make it ten,' David repeated.

'You needn't worry about clearing anything up. I'll send another man. . . .'

'I've got something I particularly want to do. I won't be available before ten.'

'But, Carr,' Carey began again; he sounded a good deal less confident than usual, and David was aware of it.

'I'll chance it,' David said.

'Oh very well.'

Carey sounded more than a little injured.

David put the receiver down, discovering that he was grinning. There was indeed something he particularly wanted to do: he wasn't going to leave without telling Jala. He had a message for her.

He began to calculate. If he rose at five instead of six he could just about get to the Valley and back again. . . . But if he had a puncture, he thought, if the jeep broke down . . .

He would go now, this minute. Action this day. He fetched a sweater from his bedroom, the smile broadening as he walked to the office building. He found a jeep, but it was locked. Around him, in the almost shadowless stare of the arc lamps, men were still working and would continue throughout the night. They were craftsmen, Comingi, earning overtime and loving it. Not a Kambla was in sight. At six precisely they stopped such work as they were doing. Nothing would tempt them. It took a little time to find the driver. David had the tank filled and the tyres checked. He took the key from the driver, declining with a smile his offer to accompany him. The driver was another Comingo, tall, courteous without subservience. David drove away. The night was hotter than ever.

He fought his way up the track in the dubious light of the jeep's headlamps. He was thinking that if he was going to do much more of this, then really he must put a proper light on one of the jeeps. He was thinking, too, of Mr Martin. Mr Martin had said that to send Jala to England, even to Paris for a little, had been a gamble. David supposed that it had been, though it was difficult to imagine Jala refined by the rigours of an English girls' school, impossible to think of her unsexed by urban airs. That was because it hadn't happened. It had been a gamble all right, but Mr Martin had won it. Jala was still Jala. She was a beauty and she was a woman.

David left the jeep at the mouth of the Valley again. He walked to Mr Martin's house and Jala opened to him. 'I'm going to England,' he told her at once. 'Only a few days, but there'll be time to do a little shopping. Now what would you like?'

He was smiling, a little eager, certain that she would be pleased.

She leapt at him in a sort of fury; he thought that she was going to strike him. Her body came against his own with an utter abandon. He gave a pace, but he held her. She was an armful, he thought. She was sobbing. 'I shall never see you again,' she said.

'What on earth do you mean?'

'You're going away. You're going to leave me. So you think you can send me a present.'

'I'm not going to send you a present, I'm going to bring you one.'

Jala paid no attention. 'You're going to send a present,' she repeated, 'to the little Cominga.'

David was conscious of a moment of irritation: it was something more than unfair. For an instant anger was his ally; he said what otherwise he might not; he said what first came into his head – the first and the best. 'What is a Cominga?' he asked. 'Tell me that, since you throw it at me.'

He put his hands on Jala's shoulders, pushing her from him. He looked at her and his heart turned over. She was weeping, but the tears hadn't destroyed her. He shook her quite sharply. 'Never again say that,' he said. 'Never.' He looked at her once more. So this was a Cominga. He was furious with her; he had never before considered it.

Jala was a little quieter now. She took the ghost of a handkerchief from a pocket in her skirt; she even contrived a smile. But her next question astonished him. 'Is she fairer than I?' she asked. It came quite without warning.

'No,' David said. He knew what Jala meant: it wouldn't be any good pretending with her. 'No,' he repeated.

It was literally true. Margaret Harrison was a Celt. In no sense was she fairer.

'She's cleverer, I suppose.'

'Perhaps. But she isn't wiser.'

'Can she bear you stronger sons?'

'I shouldn't think so.'

David saw that he couldn't draw back.

'Nor love you better?'

'No,' David said. He was sure about that.

Jala was against him again, and again she was weeping – not wildly now, but quietly, bitterly. It was very hard to bear. David tried to comfort her, but she would not raise her head. Finally she drew away, looking at him steadily, searching him. She stood erect, almost as tall as he, free and magnificent. Her splendid bosom rose with her breathing. David thought she was superb. 'You shall not leave me alone,' she said.

He did not at once understand her. She stamped her foot. 'Am I a hag?' she asked. 'Are you not a man?'

'I'm a man,' David said after a moment. He was more conscious of it than he could remember.

'Then prove it.'

David was miserable. He told himself that he was behaving very well and – and he felt a worm. Women could do that to you, he reflected; they could mostly put you in the wrong. The better you liked one ... Jala thought him less than a man; she wouldn't give him credit that he was behaving like a man's pale imitation, like a gentleman. The word was meaningless. 'I suppose,' he said unhappily, 'I suppose it's no good saying that your father is my friend?'

Jala stamped her foot again, imperially; she said something in Comingo about Mr Martin. It was notably short of dutiful.

David held out his hand, but Jala did not take it. She was looking at the sky and she was smiling again. 'It is going to rain,' she said composedly, 'and very soon.'

David followed her glance upward. A mutter of thunder seconded her. The stars had disappeared. 'I shall have to hurry,' he said.

'You will. But you won't get home.'

'Nonsense. The track will go, of course, but I can leave the jeep and send for it. I'll go by footpath.'

Jala laughed at him. 'Have you seen the footpath,' she asked, 'after rain – heavy rain? That's what we're in for, you know. When it rains, up here in the Valley. . . . It takes days, sometimes.'

David was silent, looking at the sky again. The heavens split in a sudden vivid weal. There was a moment of terrifying tension resolved by the thunder. It rolled round the bowl of hills interminably. The enormous rain began and in a second they were soaking.

Jala was laughing again; she took his hand. 'Come in, David,' she said. She hadn't called him David before.

'No,' David said. He laughed shortly. The sound of it did not please him, but the effect on Jala, animal-sharp, was immediate. In an instant she had accepted. 'Will you not come in?' she asked again. She had become the considerate, the well-bred hostess. It was raining and a visitor was getting very wet. . . .

David would not sleep in the house itself, and Jala brought rugs and an oil-stove to the little outhouse, smoothing the straw, reasonable in what he knew she thought was a lunacy, quietly competent. She was polite, a little on her dignity, but nothing of resentment escaped her. David had never felt so small.

The hut wasn't uncomfortable – David had slept much harder – and the rain, its first vigour diminishing, lulled him. But it was a very long time before he slept.

It was still dark when Jala roused him. She brought rice and fried bananas and eggs and coffee. 'It's stopped raining,' she announced.

They sat together in the clean straw, eating. Presently Jala said: 'I don't understand you, David.'

'You mustn't try. It's something . . . '

'But I do mind. I mind very much.'

'Mind what, darling?'

'Not seeing you again, of course.'

David took her hand. 'You're talking nonsense,' he said.

'I don't think so.'

'I'll be back,' David said. It sounded very trite, like a melodramatic general in defeat. But he repeated himself. 'I'll be back,' he said again. He could think of nothing better.

Jala smiled and kissed him. He realized with a pang that she didn't believe a word.

He pulled himself to his feet, glancing at his watch. Jala was entirely quiet again. 'Yes,' she said, 'you mustn't miss the aeroplane.'

They walked to the jeep and David started it. He wasn't at all sure that he could take it down the hill, but he had decided that walking he would inevitably be late. He turned to Jala beside the jeep. '*Au revoir*, my love.'

'Goodbye. My heart goes with you.'

David, deliberately, climbed down from the driving seat. He caught Jala against him, kissing her fiercely. Now she was crying again, but almost silently, in a kind of resignation. It was unbearable. 'Goodbye,' she said.

'If you say that again I shall beat you. When I come back, do you hear me? When I return.'

David climbed once more into the jeep. He drove away, not looking back.

It was clear that with an hour's more rain the aircraft couldn't have landed at all. As it was, the biplane slithered in the surface mud, dipping and swaying perilously. David squelched towards it, and a man appeared from nowhere. He was carrying a shirt and a pair of drill trousers. The shirt had been washed very carefully, the trousers were faultlessly ironed. 'I return your clothes,' Telemann said, 'with many thanks.'

'Not at all.'

Telemann began to turn his black hat in his hands. David hadn't seen him do that before. 'I hear you're going to England.'

'You hear things,' David said shortly.

'It is my business.' Telemann hesitated; he was evidently embarrassed. 'You must not assume that you will be safer in England than here,' he said at length.

‘I’m not running away, my friend.’

‘I know it. If you thought I was suggesting such a thing I have been clumsy. I must apologize. I do so.’

David was silent.

‘My masters have a very long arm,’ Telemann said. ‘Collectively.’

‘If it can reach to London it must be very long indeed.’

‘It is.’

Telemann turned his hat again. ‘You are not helping me. What I suppose I am saying is that when it comes to your death I would greatly prefer to arrange it myself. I would not have you killed unbecomingly.’

‘That is very kind of you.’

Telemann sighed. ‘I am failing, really,’ he said. ‘I am failing in the principles which I have accepted; I am being more than a little disloyal in warning you. But I owe you some consideration. I owe you that you die decently. I owe you a drink or two.’

‘I hope there will be more when I return,’ David said politely.

He climbed into the little biplane and they began to taxi away. He looked from the window for Telemann, but he had disappeared.

Chapter Five

Lord Brasted had insisted that Edward Carr should see David before he did so himself. In another man the courtesy could have been overdone, could have been more than a little irritating; but Lord Brasted never irritated except intentionally. He had spent his young manhood in a climate of opinion where it wasn't enough to do something superlatively well: you must also make it look easy even if you had to stay up all night at it. He was exceptionally considerate, wholly generous, but he contrived the impression that he would die before he let you believe he was either.

Now David was talking to Edward. They had always been at ease with each other; they had shaken hands and come at once to business. 'What's the real story?' Edward had asked.

David smiled, thinking that for a politician his brother had the singular virtue of directness. 'I don't think it's particularly complicated,' he said. 'There's the promise of a raft of oil on a disputed island. Laramonda would like it and so should we. There are overtones, of course. . . .'

'Such, for instance, as the fact that Eeles is as wet as they come?'

'You said it first.'

'Or that with the political atmosphere as it is I am myself under suspicion of being something of an old-fashioned Imperialist. I have colleagues who consider me a sort of strong man *manqué*.'

David looked surprised. 'I didn't know it was as bad as that.'

Edward Carr grimaced. 'Perhaps I exaggerate,' he conceded, 'but the truth is somewhere between us.' He lit a cigarette, reflecting for some time. 'And on a personal basis?' he inquired at length. 'Brasted seems to have great confidence in you.'

'About these Kamblas, you mean? I think I can handle them.'

'Evidently so does Brasted.'

David shrugged. 'If you're asking me why, I can only guess. You can analyse this sort of thing to death. A great many people do, and it gets you nowhere. At bottom I suppose it's because though Kamblas are nominally human beings they are also rather intelligent animals. They have an animal's instincts. Plenty of people like animals, but an individual animal isn't interested in that. And plenty of people ooze sympathy for the Kamblas – Eeles does for one. ... The Kamblas – that's the point, if there is one: an abstraction. There's a vast literature of protest about the Untouchables, for instance, the underprivileged, whatever that may mean, the unemployable – what have you. The Kamblas don't think like that and as it happens nor do I.'

'I think I see,' Edward Carr said slowly.

'Not that I *like* them as individuals,' David went on a little apologetically. 'As individuals they are detestable. I've pushed them around as much as the next man. One has to, you know. Let us leave it that one advantage of having taught professionally is that one soon loses the academic approach.'

Edward Carr laughed. 'All right,' he said. 'Abstractions, people in groups and classes under somebody else's definition. ... It's exceedingly fashionable, though. Obviously Clementi will play his hand that way.'

'He's started to.'

'So I hear.'

'This man Telemann ...'

'You've met him?'

'He called on me formally. Later, as you know, Carey had him beaten up. A mistake. I suppose that's why I'm here. I took him in and mended him up a bit, or to be accurate I gave him the opportunity to mend himself.'

'They ought to have him by now,' Edward Carr said irritably.

'Oh, I don't know. From what they told me in the Colony, Eeles isn't exactly rearing to pull him in. And for once he might be right. Arrest and deport him, and you may force Clementi's hand. Which I gather you're not ready to do. Or if Clementi didn't fly off the handle, Telemann, like all his kind, is expendable. Somebody else would arrive.'

'It's extremely unsatisfactory,' the Minister said unhappily.

'Of course it is.'

'It puts you in a spot.'

'On the spot,' David said.

'What do you mean?'

'Telemann is nothing if not candid.'

'You mean he threatened you?'

'Of course he did.'

'I'll be damned.'

'I shouldn't wonder. But on the supposition that I could stand in the way of his plans with the Kamblas . . . '

Edward Carr interrupted. 'When?' he inquired crisply. 'And what?'

David suppressed a smile. This was the Minister and no nonsense. 'He called on me to begin with,' he said, 'as I told you. He made it very clear that it might be him or me. Later, when I intervened in that stupid affair of Carey's he insisted that my helping him couldn't make any difference. He's a gentleman, you know. As it happens I have a suspicion who he really is. He's older, of course, and he's shaved his head, but I have a feeling I've met him.' David Carr held up his hand as his brother seemed about to interrupt. 'And finally he appeared from nowhere on the airstrip as I was leaving and warned me that I shouldn't be any safer in England than I was on St Cree's.'

The Minister's hand went out towards his telephone. 'What are you going to do?' David asked calmly.

'I'm going to have you protected, of course.'

'From what? From a bullet in the back out of a passing car? They're that sort of people, you know, whatever Telemann may be. Some plain-clothes dick padding about behind me. . . . ' David shook his head. 'Waste of time,' he said curtly. 'They're professionals.'

'But my dear fellow! Here – in England . . . '

'If they really mean to kill me they can do it here as easily as on St Cree's.'

'You're joking.'

'I wish I were.'

'Christ,' said Edward Carr; he considered carefully. 'I shall pass this on,' he added at length. 'I am obliged to. The details are not for me.'

'I couldn't object to that.'

'I wouldn't mind if you did,' the Secretary of State said coolly.

They sat for some time in an understanding silence. The Minister broke it with a question which his brother hadn't been expecting. 'Will you be seeing Margaret?'

David concealed his surprise. 'I expect so,' he said. 'It would be rather rude not to. I thought I'd ask her to dinner.'

'Good luck, then.'

David opened his mouth and shut it again; he was ready – very ready, he realized – to think about Jala, but not yet to discuss her. He looked at his watch, and his brother took the hint. He rose. 'Lunch-time,' he said in brief acceptance. 'Where shall we go?'

David had been dining with Margaret Harrison; he had been glad to see her as he always was, at ease . . . and quite unexcited. She was twenty-seven at this time, though her colouring belied it; she had comfortable means but she worked. She was a journalist. Her father had not offered her the polite, the genial head-start which he could have contrived, for she would have declined it. She had started with a pencil and a writing pad and her private brand of shorthand. Now she edited a prosperous woman's paper.

And she was a damned nice woman, David thought. It was a pity she simply couldn't see things.

He sighed. At dinner Margaret had started to talk about the war. David hadn't particularly minded. It was something which was behind him by now, but he hadn't so much in common with Margaret, not so much to talk about, that he could afford to discard good material. At least the war had been incident, and incident, with Margaret, was something safe and something appreciated. She didn't care for shop or gossip. David told her about his batman.

He had been a tiny man – an inch less would have made him a midget – and why the Army had accepted him was still unexplained. He was extremely handy with high explosives, and he had done time both in England and in America. But he wasn't the sort of criminal with a grudge against society; prison he regarded as one of the vocational risks of a skilled and on the whole reasonably lucrative profession. He was a very good soldier indeed and he had a strong sense of justice. To David that was the point of the tale and he had tried to tell it accordingly.

Margaret hadn't taken it.

The two of them had been captured in one of those preposterous battles where nobody knew what was happening. David had fought in several battles which, as exercises at a Staff College, would have satisfied no instructor, but this had been something of a classic amongst muddles. What was left of his Company was being marched away under a modest escort and a rather elderly enemy officer. They had marched for about a mile when one of the men had made a break for it. Perfectly properly the enemy officer had shot at him, and he had fallen, holding his stomach. Perfectly improperly the enemy officer had then walked to him where he lay and blown his brains out. The British stood silent and frozen, their hands closing and unclosing. They marched on miserably and suddenly, for no reason apparent, an American tank was rolling along the road towards them, its machine guns traversing the little party in silent menace. The escort dropped their arms and the tank stopped. From its hatch climbed an American captain. He was lean and sallow and dangerous, and his face was entirely expressionless. He saluted David Carr and walked along the little line of exhausted men; he stopped at David's orderly; he held out his hand. 'Hiya Shorty?' he inquired.

'Hiya Mike.'

There followed a rapid exchange in an argot which David had imperfectly followed. His orderly jerked his thumb at the enemy officer. 'So?' said the sallow Captain. 'So?' He turned his formidable deadpan upon the enemy officer. His pale grey eyes were as cold as ice. He returned to David's orderly. 'Care for me to push him?' he asked.

'Nope. I'll do him myself.'

'O.K. by me.'

The sallow Captain spun his automatic at the orderly. He spun it, carefully, anti-clockwise, and the butt came into the orderly's hand as neatly as if it had been dropped there. Simultaneously his thumb slid the safety catch. The sallow Captain moved two paces to his left. Now he was between David and the enemy officer. He produced a gold cigarette-case, and his speech changed instantly into the accents of the Harvard Club. 'May I offer you a cigarette, sir,' he inquired. 'Luckies to the left,' he said, 'and Players to the right,' he added unexpectedly. David took a Player; he bent his head to the lighter which the sallow Captain held for him. There was a report, and another. He lifted his head, exhaling blissfully. The enemy officer was lying in the ditch. He was evidently very dead. The orderly was back in the ranks. The pistol, magically, was back in the American's holster. Nobody had said a word.

The sallow Captain turned to what was left of the escort. 'Beat it,' he said briefly. 'Scram.' He accompanied the words with a wide gesture, and the escort melted silently into the fields. 'I can't take prisoners,' he explained. 'Here on business, you know. The radio says there's some rubbish retreating down this road and we've come for a crack at it.' He waved at his tank and at the wood behind him. 'Myself and three others,' he added, 'and something rather special in the way of a recoil-less.' He looked at David Carr again; he looked at his scar and he looked at his left breast. 'Have you any engagements in particular? I was wondering whether you would care to join us. You won't, I hope, think it an impertinence, but there might be some interesting shooting. There's an artilleryman too, very pleased with his new toy. He would be delighted to demonstrate.'

'I should be charmed.'

'Splendid. Then perhaps we ought to be moving. May I suggest that your men keep away from the road?' The sallow Captain turned again to David's orderly. Again he held out his hand. 'See you, Shorty,' he said.

'See you, Mike,' said the orderly.

David had leant back in the restaurant chair conscious that he hadn't told the story too badly. There was something more than a coincidence about it, he considered; the affair had been something more than a lynching, there was a sort of wild equity about it, an edge. . . .

Margaret Harrison hadn't seen it. To do her justice she hadn't said anything deplorable; she hadn't said anything about two wrongs not making a right; she hadn't looked surprised, far less disapproving. But she simply hadn't seen what to David was the meat. The American Captain had struck her as a fortunate coincidence: she was a journalist, she knew that life mostly beat fiction. It was a pretty good tale and she would remember it.

David sighed again, thinking once more that she was a damned nice woman. Once he had nearly proposed. If he married her, then for better or worse his household would be run superbly, his children would have beautiful manners, he would be considered as he grew older. It would be a splendid match, an alliance even. . . .

He simply didn't want her.

He put his car into its garage and walked towards the hotel. He had found a short cut through an alley and another mews. At this hour it was ill-lighted, but he knew the way.

He was aware that in the dark mews three men were upon him. They were masked. He saw that one had a pistol and another a knife. The third had that thing. Instinctively he backed against the wall, realizing that he was just too late. The man was already behind him, and his stomach fell into a sickening nothing as he felt the wire around his neck. Somehow he forced himself to stand still. He had used that thing himself; he knew that upon the wire would be a pawl and a ratchet, devilish, unbreakable. Once it was on you you died. You died silently, unspeakably – clawing like an animal. He had seen it. . . . He forced himself to stand still. Move and there would be that fatal jerk. You would die horribly – death, when it came, a release. But sometimes, they had taught you, sometimes a garrotter became over-confident; he moved that bare half-pace too close. . . .

David felt the man's body against his own. He threw back his arm and the man's head came into the crook of it. He had practised it, at Unarmed Combat, a hundred times. He threw his body forward, and the man swung around his shoulder. For a moment David caught his expression in the half-light; it was surprised rather than fearful. The man came round his shoulder a little further as he straightened. His feet were in the air and his legs were splaying. David raised his knee and the man fell into the little gutter of the mews, clutching at himself, screaming.

David did not bother to look at him. He turned to the second man, the man with the knife. He knows his business, he told himself. The knife was held low, point upwards: the blow would come upwards too, into the stomach. You would live a little, but not pleasantly. The man began to move. I am for it, David thought. He dropped his left forearm deliberately upon the knife. He felt it sear the flesh; grind horribly against the bone. The heel of his right hand thudded against the second man's jaw. It was only in books and at the pictures that people hit each other with the naked fist. You merely broke your fingers if you did. He heard the man's tiny gasp as his knees gave under him. He fell quite slowly, sliding down David's body; he fell upon his face. David raised his right foot. The toe was up, as he had been taught, and the heel down. He measured the distance. He dropped his heel precisely upon the other's neck.

He turned towards the last. It was a revolver, he saw, and there was supposed to be a way of catching a revolver, by the chambers, so that . . . They had been at pains to impress on you that it was a convention of a certain sort of cinema; in practice it didn't do; it didn't do at all. Come to think of it, nothing did very much against a man with a firearm who knew enough to keep a proper distance. David Carr bent down; he picked up the knife and began to walk slowly towards the third man. His arm came up and there was a flash and bang. It was too close to hear the bullet. David walked on in an agony, not hoping. He could see the man's face now and, under the eye-mask, it looked incredulous. His arm had dropped and now it came up again. David was almost upon him. He turned quite suddenly and he began to run. David ran after him. He found that he could not. He dropped the knife. He stood in the little mews, his feet widely planted, bellowing wordlessly, bellowing at the retreating gunman, roaring in an animal rage. He took the wire, still loose, from around his neck and looked at it. 'Bloody thing,' he said aloud. 'Bloody, bastard thing.'

Two men appeared, running, at the mouth of the mews. One wore a cap and the other a bowler hat. Bowler hat had a suit-case. They came to David Carr. 'My God,' said cap, 'we thought we'd lost you.'

'And our jobs,' said bowler hat. He caught at David as he staggered. 'Steady.' Bowler hat looked at David's arm. Blood had already seeped through the sleeve of the overcoat. Bowler hat produced a razor and a first-aid pack. With movements of surprising neatness he cut away the sleeves of both overcoat and jacket. The shirt was stuck to the arm, and bowler hat removed it delicately. He looked at the wound. 'Nasty,' he said. 'Quite nasty. Lucky it was outside.' He began, expertly, to bandage over a pad. 'This will hold it for a bit. Then hospital, of course. We'll have an ambulance in a minute.' He split the end of the bandage and tied it quickly. 'Nothing else?' he inquired. 'We heard a shot.'

'He missed,' David said. 'He got away.'

'Lucky again.'

Cap was examining the man in the gutter. His screaming, now, had diminished to a gasping groan. He still jerked convulsively, and he still held himself together. Cap went behind him, running his hands over his body. 'Clean,' he said. The garrotter made an effort to rise. Cap pushed him down again. He took off his mask and he shook his head, turning to bowler hat. 'Know him, Tom?' he asked.

Bowler hat left David for a moment and inspected the garrotter. He shook his head in turn. 'No, he's new to me.'

Cap turned to David. 'Rough,' he said reflectively, 'a

little rough perhaps. But undeniably effective.' He spoke in the unemotional tone of one professional man assessing the work of another.

He crossed to the second man and again ran his hands over him. The man with the knife was still upon his face, motionless. Cap rolled him over, examining him again more carefully. He felt his pulse and he put his ear on his breast. Finally he held a pocket mirror before his mouth. 'He seems to be alive,' he said conversationally. 'Just.' He turned to bowler hat. 'Better call 'em up,' he added shortly.

Bowler hat walked to the suit-case which he had left to bandage David. He opened it and displayed a portable transmitter. He pulled a knob and an extensible aerial rose from a corner. Bowler hat spoke briefly, apparently satisfied. 'Cars will be here in five minutes,' he announced. 'And an ambulance.'

Cap produced cigarettes and the three men lit up. He jerked his thumb at the man in the gutter, turning to bowler hat. 'I've never liked the wire,' he said, 'but oughtn't we to do something?'

Bowler hat appeared to consider this. 'He won't run away,' he said finally. He looked again at the garrotter, still writhing. 'He won't run away,' he repeated coolly. 'He can't.'

'I suppose not. . . . ' Cap addressed himself to David Carr. 'You seem to have done pretty well, sir, if I may say so. Three of them – armed. . . . There will be explanations, of course. Awkward ones, I imagine, for somebody. But don't try and talk now.'

'Thank you.'

'A doctor is what you need. About six stitches, I should say. A doctor and a cup of tea. With something in it. We'll get the other one, of course.'

A police car and an ambulance backed into the mews. David, on Cap's arm, walked to the door. He turned with his foot on the step. Two men were putting the garrotter on to a stretcher. They were careful and they were expert. But as they moved him he screamed again.

David woke next morning in what he recognized as a room in a nursing home. His arm was bandaged and very stiff, but it did not hurt him. He was grateful for that, for he had suffered enough pain to have no illusions about his dignity. A bellpush hung above his head and he reached for it. A starched little nurse brought tea, and David asked for his cigarette-case. He drank the tea and smoked two cigarettes. All of them tasted delicious.

He relaxed again in the cool sheets, stretching like a dog. He suspected that whatever anaesthetic had been given him hadn't entirely worn off; that he was still a little dopey. But this euphoria wasn't merely chemical. Life was extraordinarily simple again, uncertainty a word without meaning. He hadn't felt like this since – since the war, he told himself, smiling. Now, as then, there was only one David Carr, and now there were only two things which he wanted to do. The first would be pleasurable and the omens were happy. It was to marry Jala. The second would be more difficult, though it was at least as important. It was to kill Telemann.

Telemann ... David was certain that he had met him before. It was there, at the back of his mind, but he couldn't pin it. Telemann – it wasn't a Spanish name at all. . . .

Now why was he thinking about Spain?

Not that it mattered, David decided. He stretched again drowsily. Not that it mattered. He would have to kill him.

Unless, of course, they got him first. Evidently they weren't people to take lightly.

Chapter Six

Edward Carr had decided that he spent a disproportionate amount of time reading the dispatches of Sir Francis Eeles. Such information, such hard news as they gave him he obtained from other sources: sometimes Lord Brasted told him, and sometimes he simply read it in his morning newspaper. And the Governor's comment he could by now almost write for himself. Always it was sane; invariably it walked straight down what Sir Francis imagined was the middle of the road. Occasionally these dispatches came as near to the impertinent as made no difference, though His Excellency would have been horrified if he had known that his Minister so thought them. This the Minister realized. He smiled a little grimly, thinking that intellectual arrogance was very difficult to conceal.

He read the latest dispatch with distaste. It told him that there were now adequate police upon St Cree's – adequate, that is, to look after the enormously swollen population. Whether they were adequate to deal with trouble Sir Francis did not say, for Sir Francis wasn't a man to talk of trouble before it was breathing on his neck. A resident magistrate had also been detailed; he would arrive as soon as suitable accommodation had been arranged. Universal had very kindly agreed to provide it. The Minister smiled again. But these police had not yet been able to arrest the man Telemann. He seemed extremely elusive, which could only mean that he wasn't without sympathizers. The Governor made the point with some emphasis; evidently he wasn't living for Telemann's arrest. If he was found, then of course he could be deported for illegal entry. But it was clear that his arrest would be something decisive, a crisis perhaps, and Sir Francis Eeles . . .

Sir Francis Eeles had thought it worth while pointing out that if Telemann were deported Clementi could always send another man.

Edward Carr dropped the Savingram into his tray. The gesture expressed his opinion of it. He crossed to his safe and took from it another paper. It hadn't been prepared by any of his own staff, nor had he any intention of letting them see it. Not even his Under-Secretary of State – particularly not his Under-Secretary of State. The document wasn't headed, and it was typed on perfectly plain foolscap. It wasn't signed. The Minister began to read it, rather quickly at first, for the niceties of military appreciation, to say nothing of its jargon, were a little beyond him. But the last two paragraphs he read twice:

5. All this proceeds upon two assumptions:
(i) that it would in practice be possible to reinforce the Colony without forcing Clementi into open hostilities before we had reached something approaching parity with him, and
(ii) that any hostilities could be localized.
6. Clementi has no potential ally in the area worth consideration. His potential Ally elsewhere is known.

At the bottom of this paper was written, and in pencil: 'And if they came in your guess would be as good as mine. If any of us were here to guess.'

The Minister read these paragraphs for the third time. They depressed him. He locked the paper in his safe again and returning to his desk, took from a drawer a booklet rather indifferently printed. It was headed *Her Majesty*'s *Ministers and Heads of Public Departments*. Its price was carefully recorded as 'One Shilling Net – Postal Subscription

Six-and-Sixpence for Six Issues'. It began with the Prime Minister. He had a whole line to himself. Then came the Cabinet; then Ministers Not in the Cabinet; finally, faint but hopeful, the Law Officers.

Edward Carr counted quickly – with the Prime Minister the Cabinet was nineteen. Not that that was the effective body, he reflected: there was an inner Cabinet of six or perhaps seven. He wasn't a member of it. But the Cabinet, formally and constitutionally, was himself and eighteen others.

He took a pencil and began to mark the list. He put against the nineteen names five pluses, six minuses, and eight noughts. He was applying an admirably simple test: not what a man would do under threat of war – Edward Carr would have considered that unrealistic. The threat of war could come in a dozen forms and in circumstances incalculable. Allies could be unreliable. . . . Not the threat of war then, but something much more homely. Edward Carr was deciding which of his colleagues would resign, throw overboard his personal ambitions, rather than lose an oilfield to a potential enemy. The pluses were men who would do so, the minuses those who would not. The noughts were undecided. It was a test of men not of policies.

Edward Carr wasn't a very clever man, but he had something more useful than intelligence. He could smell a quitter at a mile.

Five and six and eight, he thought – it wasn't too good. Well, there was something he could do: he could talk to the Foreign Secretary. The Foreign Secretary was in the inner ring, and he was a natural ally. Unhappily he was also a nought.

Unhappily, too, Edward Carr had no great opinion of Her Majesty's Principal Secretary of State for Foreign Affairs. That was his proper title and he was attached to it; he particularly disliked being referred to as the Foreign Secretary. But Edward Carr considered that the resounding rubric concealed something of an ass. Rather a surprising kind of ass at that. For here was a man with everything – money and lineage and, by marriage, a great political family behind him. You would have expected flair, perhaps the grand manner: at least you would have expected expertise. But the Foreign Secretary didn't honour expectations at all. Even his appearance was a disappointment. A tall man would have been in order, lean and ascetic; or, if he wasn't so tall, then at least he must be leonine. What you got was a fat little bun in a body-belt which screamed to heaven. He was bald too, and something – something not very serious but quite inescapable – something was wrong with his scalp. A halo of vestigial hair crowned him above the ears. He was very unattractive indeed.

And as Her Majesty's Principal Secretary of State he was hardly a flier. He was a beaver, a delver, a master of his papers. Speaking to a Brief he was impeccable. He was an excellent Chairman, a step-by-stepper. He loved a Conference and he worshipped an Agreement; he would concede almost anything for a formal agreement on paper. He would have made an admirable Permanent Under-Secretary to a genuine Minister.

Edward Carr mistrusted him, but he knew that he could not be ignored. The House wasn't sitting, and he knew where the Foreign Secretary could be found; he could be found in his room at the Foreign Office; he would be studying the papers. It probably wasn't necessary to make an appointment, but Edward Carr was a courteous man and he did so. He put on his hat and walked to Downing Street.

He was shown to the Foreign Secretary's room at once. It was empty, but a polite private secretary was there to reassure him. . . . The Foreign Secretary would be back almost immediately. Edward Carr looked around him. He was a politician as well as a Minister, and he began to think politically. He had always thought it rather a fine room. It was bigger than his own, grander and with a better view. His own room looked on to nothing in particular, whereas from here there was a view of Horse Guards. Damn it, you could see the Troopings; you could invite visitors; and there must be a dozen other rooms with views almost as good. Say a dozen rooms at your disposal and five visitors to the room. That was sixty visitors, sixty constituents, sixty votes. . . .

The Foreign Secretary came in quickly. He smiled, showing dubious teeth. 'I needn't waste time by inquiry,' he said at once. 'It must be about St Cree's.'

'It is.'

'I feel reasonably confident about that. I think we can block Clementi's claims where it matters.'

'I had rather assumed that,' Edward Carr said levelly; he lit the cigarette which he had not been offered. 'But I am rather less confident about St Cree's itself. There is at least the possibility of serious trouble locally.'

The Foreign Secretary looked deliberately blank; he was trying, too, not to look shocked, like a family doctor, Carr thought, told by paterfamilias that he required a peculiarly specialist attention. 'St Cree's is British territory,' the Foreign Secretary said finally. 'It is hardly my bailiwick.'

'I concede it. Would you concede that I should put troops on it?'

The Foreign Secretary put the tips of his fingers together; he did not answer directly, for he seldom did. 'You will understand,' he began, 'that if troops were to land on St Cree's the non-militarization agreement . . . '

But Edward Carr interrupted. 'Precisely,' he said. 'I ask you the question only to establish our common interest.'

The Foreign Secretary accepted this with a smile; he had intended it to be gracious, but in the event it was a little superior. 'There is this oil,' he said vaguely. He did not sound gratified that it existed.

'Sterling oil,' Carr said.

'Ah . . . Ah, yes.' The Foreign Secretary began to explain

about Sterling oil. 'The term,' he said, 'is decidedly misleading. There is Sterling in Dollar oil, as you know, and a Dollar content even in Sterling oil. The arrangements which the companies have made internationally . . . '

'Quite so. But we may take it, I think, that Sterling oil is still a great deal preferable to any other.'

'I suppose so,' the Foreign Secretary said. He made the admission with an evident reluctance.

'And that its loss would be very serious politically?'

'I am afraid so.' The Foreign Secretary sounded more reluctant than ever.

'Then putting it at its crudest the object of this visit is to ask you how far you will go with me.'

The Foreign Secretary shifted on his chair. 'In what direction?' he asked uneasily. He was sparring.

'In the direction of keeping this oil for this country.'

The Foreign Secretary relaxed; he felt that he was over the hump. 'That,' he said precisely, 'that would surely be a Cabinet decision.'

Edward Carr gazed from the other window on to St James's Park. He was disappointed but in no way surprised. The interview was at an end and he was aware of it. But he did not move. There was one other thing which he wanted to know; he could not ask it, but there was a chance that the Foreign Secretary would give it away. He sat on quietly.

Presently the Foreign Secretary began to talk again, making conversation in a situation which embarrassed him, talking, as Edward Carr had hoped he might, a little at random. 'This is a very difficult position,' he said. 'The local complications . . . ' His voice tailed away.

'We are pretty well informed about the local complications,' Carr said. This wasn't going too badly; there was a chance. . . .

'Ah, yes. Of course. Eeles would report more than adequately.'

'Exactly.'

'A very sound man I always thought him when he was in Whitehall. We had quite a lot to do with him. An excellent appointment. Yes, a very sound man indeed.'

Edward Carr had been told what he wished to discover, but his expression did not change. So that was how it lay.... He rose to his feet. 'Thank you very much,' he said. 'You have been very helpful.' He was lying and he knew it.

'Not at all. At any time ... '

Edward Carr walked from the Foreign Office, glancing at his watch. He was a little late for his visit to David. He had seen him only once since the nursing home, rather a strict one, had swallowed him, and then only shortly. Now he wanted to talk; now he was surprised as well as a little annoyed to find that Lord Brasted was before him. The two men were sitting in a total silence, and that was unusual. Lord Brasted, in his time, had had most adjectives applied to him, but nobody had ever suggested that he wasn't articulate. His numerous enemies said that he was a garrulous old man. Yet here he was sitting in silence, a comfortable, a positive thing....

Edward Carr found himself wondering what he had to be silent about.

Lord Brasted rose politely as he entered. 'I hope I'm not intruding,' he said. 'I was bringing your brother a little news.'

'Really?' Edward Carr was trying not to sound irritated.

'Yes, I think so. Those men a couple of nights ago, you know. One of them is still at large, but the other two have been identified. They slipped across from the Continent a week ago, and they have precisely the connexions you would have expected.'

The Minister, now, was seriously annoyed. 'I hadn't been told that,' he said sharply.

'You will be, my dear fellow. As soon as you get back to your office, I shouldn't wonder.'

'Damn it, James, your information seems to be better than my own.'

'Not better,' Lord Brasted said coolly. 'Just a little quicker.' He waved his hand, dismissing the matter. 'You must remember that I pay a good deal of money for it.'

The Secretary of State achieved a smile; he considered for some time. 'Well,' he said finally, 'that decides one thing at least. It is impossible for David to return.'

The two heads turned to him together.

'No,' Brasted said.

'No,' said David.

'What do you mean, "No"?'

'I mean,' David said, 'that I'm going back to St Cree's.'

Edward Carr looked at Lord Brasted and Lord Brasted returned his inspection. 'I should make my own position clear,' he said calmly. 'I came here with the same thought as your own: that if your brother is the object of an organized intention to murder him, a plan which can reach even into this country, then clearly it would be unsafe for him to return to the Colony, and anybody who suggested it would be accepting a responsibility which I for one am not ready to. Not that I used the word unsafe to your brother, for I am not a fool. But I think I made my point. Your brother was a little brusque with me. So I went rather further, since it was upon my conscience that I should do so. I offered him promotion in my Company, and at home. He laughed at me.'

'But the inquiries,' Edward Carr said a little weakly, 'the trial. . . .'

'My very dear Edward, we can forget the trial. These men have been – well, let us say that it will be a month at least before they are what they were. If that were a desirable end, which I admit it is not. There could be a preliminary hearing before a magistrate I dare say, especially if the police pick up the other man. Which I am inclined to doubt – he is probably away by now. David could go to any remand proceedings if necessary, but trial . . . ' Lord Brasted shrugged. 'And apart from the fact that these men are in no condition to stand trial for some time, there is the consideration that the police are probably in no great hurry to bring one on. There will be inquiries to be made – exhaustive inquiries, if I may coin a phrase. They are on to something, something considerable, and they will want to pursue it.' Lord Brasted waved his hand again. 'David could be home in a matter of hours by air.'

'You seem very keen,' Edward Carr said acidly.

'But that is most unfair. It is unworthy. I have just explained that I have not asked your brother to return: on the contrary I have offered him a sizeable inducement not to. He declined it. And in the circumstances of your last comment I feel entitled to make one of my own. It is that I entirely understand.'

'And what do you understand?'

'I understand your brother.'

Edward Carr looked at David. He had taken no part in these exchanges; he was sitting in a dressing gown, his hands upon his knees. They were curious hands, lean and finely formed, a little delicate; but they ended in the spatulate pads of decision, they ended in unambiguous action.

'David,' Edward asked unhappily, 'I take it you realize the position? Brasted told me a week or two ago that he thought you were the man with the best chance of controlling the situation on St Cree's. Apart from this business of the Kamblas he wasn't particularly explicit – he often isn't. But that doesn't matter now, for his reasons aren't important. What is important is that other people evidently share them. They share them so strongly that they intend to kill you. They've already had one very good try at it – here in England. David – you're not simply being stubborn?'

David smiled. 'Perhaps,' he said. 'But it isn't entirely that.'

'What else then?'

'I'm going back to the island.'

Edward Carr sighed; he looked at Lord Brasted, and his expression was sadly short of friendly. Brasted had retreated again into silence. He sat there solidly, in no way in triumph, but apart, in a sort of . . . Damn it, Edward thought, it *was* a sort of understanding. James Robertson, the Viscount Brasted and the first of them, knew something of David which his brother did not. Edward Carr remembered that a week or two before Lord Brasted had been telling him that David and himself had much in common. At the time it had struck him as rather a pointless remark, as one of Brasted's little paradoxes. Well, now he was learning better; he was edging towards answering his original question, towards discovering what Lord Brasted had to be silent about.

The Minister rose with another sigh. 'I'll come again tomorrow,' he told David. 'There doesn't seem much else today.' He faced Lord Brasted for the final time. 'But,' he added grimly, 'I wish I had arrived a trifle earlier this afternoon.'

'Until tomorrow then,' David said.

Lord Brasted picked up his hat. 'I'll come with you,' he said. 'If I may.'

They went down the steps of the nursing home. Lord Brasted's Rolls was waiting and they climbed into it. 'Can I drop you?' he inquired.

'At the Office, please. If you would.'

They did not speak again.

In Great Smith Street Edward Carr thanked Lord Brasted a little stiffly. He went to his room, and at once an official was upon him with a sealed envelope. He slit it deliberately, for he could guess from the seal what it contained. . . . David's two assailants had indeed been identified. They had come from the Continent a week or so ago, and their background, their associations, were both expected and ominous. They were associations, unprovable but clear, with Clementi's Ally.

The Secretary of State took his list from the drawer again. He rubbed out the nought against the name of Her Majesty's Principal Secretary of State for Foreign Affairs and put a minus; he thought very carefully, then altered two more noughts to minuses; he counted again. . . . Five and nine and five now – worse than ever. Nine to five for scuttle, and five undecided. At best it was going to be uncomfortably close.

Edward Carr slept very badly that night; he was worried by his Cabinet arithmetic and he was worried about his brother. There was something. . . . He knew that David was a brave man, but he knew something else about brave men: they were notably unamorous of danger as such. David might be stubborn – Edward Carr more than suspected it. But he wasn't a fool.

The Minister woke finally as the morning began to lighten between the blinds. He knew that he would not sleep again, and he rose and looked from the window. It was a cold, an impersonal light, the light which assayed courage. The attack at dawn, he thought, horrible and magnificent. He looked again at the increasing dawn, and five men walked in his mind into an empty field – two principals, two seconds. They walked with formality and a grim fortitude. The Cartel read by the fifth. The Irish Code, naturally. Five men . . . and four would return alive.

Edward Carr whistled softly. He put on a dressing gown and walked, very slowly, to the bathroom. So that was it! There was strong blood on the Border still and a Black Douglas in the Carrs'. Christ! Not that David against Telemann would be a decent thing, a right and a privilege to be shared. That wasn't contemporary at all; it wasn't contemporary to stake an individual's life upon an individual's opinion of honour. Instead men fought in shapeless armies; bombed cities to saturation. And Telemann had reached for the weapons of the gutter: David, since these weapons were deadly, might have to take them too. But at bottom it was the same thing, the same motive, one man against another.

Edward Carr climbed reflectively into his bath. He began to smile, his good humour returning. He had been a little slow, but Brasted wasn't the only man of sensibility. He had been a little slow, but that was because he had been thinking first about oil. Oil. . . . He was Secretary of State for the Colonies, oil was vital, was essential. . . .

This morning it didn't come first.

*

It was David's first outing from the nursing home, and he was dressing with something more than care; he was dressing competitively. He had remembered that Telemann, his right arm useless, had clothed himself in half an hour, and he had been obliged in that time to attend to his face in addition. David's face was unharmed and his right arm was serviceable. Against that, his left arm was in a sling. A fair target, he had decided, a fair comparison, would be about twelve minutes. He would dress in twelve minutes or concede something which he had no intention of conceding.

He dressed in eleven minutes and, humming softly, went down the stairs. He had some shopping to do – very important shopping. The porter called a taxi and David directed it to an establishment in a side street in St James's. It was a very old shop with an air of unrepentant decay; the tide of demand had left it dry, but it still sold what, of their kind, were the best, the most beautiful objects in the world. A grey old man, bent, a little despairing, received him politely. 'I want,' David said, 'a ceremonial Comingo sword.'

The old man brightened into interest. 'Now that, sir,' he

said, 'is something we haven't been asked for for years.'

'Have you got one?'

'I really don't know. I . . . '

'Could you make one?' David was feeling slightly ashamed of himself; he hadn't intended to rush the old gentleman, but he wanted that sword very badly indeed.

The shopkeeper shook his head. 'Impossible, I'm afraid, sir. The craftsmen, you know – they simply don't exist any more. The damascening alone . . . ' He shook his head again. 'Of course, sir,' he added after a moment, 'we could get you a factory one, a curio.' He spoke apologetically, with a distaste which he did not attempt to conceal.

David smiled. 'I don't want that.'

'No . . . No, of course not. I didn't really think you did. You will forgive me. . . . ' The old man inspected David, levelly but without impertinence; he scratched his chin as though coming to a decision. 'If you will excuse me for a moment, sir.' He disappeared behind a glass partition, and David could see that another old man rose from his ledger to meet him. They twittered together for a moment and returned to the shop.

The second old man bowed. In turn he inspected David. He seemed to be the senior. His manner was courteous but critical. Finally he nodded. 'By a curious coincidence, sir, a Comingo sword reached us a day or two ago.' Unmindful of logic he added blandly: 'It is a very beautiful thing indeed. You will understand that we should not wish to sell it to the first inquirer. It is not an object which we should care to part with purely as a financial transaction.' His smile was charming and a little conspiratorial.

'You are very kind,' David said hopefully.

The senior old gentleman nodded again to the other. 'Bring it, please, Mr Charles.'

The other returned, rather unsteadily, with the tremendous sword. With some difficulty he got it upon the counter. The shopkeepers stood expectantly, watching David. The stitches on the curving scabbard were almost invisible. The hilt, two-handed, innocent of guard, was ebony and ivory between bandings of silver wire.

'May I draw, sir?'

'Please do.'

Deliberately, with a drama that was conscious but perfectly proper, the old man drew the appalling weapon. It was something between a scimitar and the grandfather of all kukris. The blade was a work of the highest craftsmanship, the highest fancy. David gave a little sigh. 'Beautiful,' he said involuntarily.

'Exquisite, sir. About sixteen-ninety, I should say. A very good period. Italian, of course. Lovely. . . . And I understand by no means purely ornamental.'

'By no means purely ornamental,' David agreed.

'You can behead an ox with them, I believe.'

'You can – if you know how.'

'Most interesting. And I am told there are other ceremonial uses as well. They say that Cominga ladies marry upon them.'

'They do.'

'I am extremely curious,' the old gentleman said mildly.

David smiled. 'If you want to marry a Cominga of family, you offer her father one of these swords. If he draws the hilt an inch or two your suit is favourably received. If the lady herself pushes it back again you are married.'

'Indeed? I am most grateful, sir. I had heard something of the sort, but never, I suspect, quite rightly. A most interesting custom. . . . Idyllic, really.'

'It is convenient.'

'And dignified,' said the shopkeeper. He began to talk about dignity and its decline. David listened politely; he still wasn't quite sure that he was going to be allowed to buy. The other old man teetered away behind the partition again, returning with glasses and a decanter of sherry. Finally the senior said: 'You seem to like the blade, sir. You appreciate it.'

'I like it enormously.'

'I fear you may not like the price.'

David's eyebrows rose in inquiry, and the old man named a figure. It was a very substantial sum, but a fair one. 'I'm not carrying that, naturally. I could go to my bank or leave a cheque and call tomorrow.'

The old gentlemen looked surprised. 'I would not,' the elder said, 'sell this weapon to a customer whose cheque I could not accept.'

'Then thank you very much.'

David wrote a cheque and was bowed into a taxi. The ceremonial sword followed him. He held it between his knees, smiling happily. Two things in life he had to do, and the first would be sweet indeed. He would arrange that – he had just arranged it. Jala.... He found that his pulse was thumping, and he was delighted. Darling Jala. . . . Not Margaret, not Margaret at all. Marry Margaret and the flowers would be beautifully arranged, supper invariably punctual. The laundry would be counted. . . . It wasn't there, it simply wasn't *there*. He was thirty-six. That wasn't old, but nor was it exactly young. In five years or ten – in five years or ten it would be Margaret or somebody like her. He hadn't too much time, he owed himself that, he wasn't going to miss it, it was important....

It was important all right.

Chapter Seven

Sir Francis Eeles would probably not have believed that his Chief Secretary did not resent his appointment, for in the jargon of his Service he was a Whitehall man, and in Whitehall promotion over another's head was something very serious. It was something serious because it was everything. By the time a man had fought his way into the zone of top promotion he had fought himself out of just about everything else. To be passed over was failure; it was, and in a precise sense, death. Sir Francis, who was conventionally, excessively ambitious, certainly wouldn't have believed that Masters had accepted the position.

Though in fact he had. For Harry Masters was aware of the rules of his profession, and by those rules Eeles, the better man on paper, was the better man. It was as simple as that, and Masters was philosophical. But he also saw no reason to deceive himself. His private opinion of Sir Francis Eeles was that he was a worm and no man. In particular he lost his balance far too easily, and about matters which to Harry Masters were the stuff of adolescence.

The Governor was very cross at this moment. He was pacing the slightly improbable drawing-room of Government House, working himself into a temper. 'It's an outrage,' he was saying. 'An outrage.'

Harry Masters knew what he meant: His Excellency meant that it was an outrage to allow David Carr to return to St Cree's. 'Yes,' he said non-committally.

'I don't see how there can be two opinions. It's – it's provocation.'

'To Clementi, you mean?'

'Whom else?'

Harry Masters suppressed a smile; he was thinking that though his definition of provocation might not differ from the Governor's his application of the word decidedly would. For here was David Carr murderously set upon, almost certainly with Clementi's knowledge and probably at his instance. . . . So you allowed him to return where he could most easily be attacked again. And that was provocation – that provoked the attacker. Masters sipped his parsimonious whisky and soda, inspecting his Governor coolly, deciding that if he intended to lose his temper he might as well do it properly. He, Masters, would be delighted to help him. 'I don't know,' he said deliberately. 'Any other course would have smacked of appeasement.'

Sir Francis, as Masters had expected, exploded promptly. 'Appeasement!' he said furiously. 'A gutter word, the language of the kitchen. And meaningless. I have always resented it.'

'That I can understand,' Masters said evenly.

'The affairs of nations cannot be conducted on the principles of the fifth form.'

'I got into the seventh myself. But then I was a King's Scholar.'

This the Governor ignored. He went on pacing up and down, a little self-consciously. Masters was thinking that he wasn't a very good actor: in fact he was a bit of a ham. Sir Francis turned at the far end of the room. The pose might be melodramatic but it wasn't ineffective. 'I have never trusted Universal,' he said. 'I do not conceal that their ideas of government are not my own. They have altogether too much authority, too much power, both here and, I'm afraid, at home. They are a state within a state. That I cannot approve.'

'Evidently not.'

'This building-up of the Comingi, ignoring the Kamblas. This playing at petroleros. . . . '

'I'm not altogether sure that I agree with you about Comingi. Can you imagine Universal running its present operations on Kambla labour or even a substantial proportion of it? And after all, Comingi are extraordinarily attractive people.'

His Excellency went off again, this time unexpectedly. 'Have you ever been in India?' he inquired.

'No, I have missed that.'

'A pity,' the Governor said acidly, 'for you would find the same thing there. The average European, and I use the adjective advisedly, the average European greatly prefers the Muslim to the Hindu. The Muslim has often a better physique, his manner is more manly; he accepts a revealed religion, he is a Book Brother. There is an idea, largely romantic, I suggest, that he is more reliable. He has a sense of humour and he looks you in the eye.'

'They don't seem bad reasons for preference,' Masters said.

'By the standards of suburbia they are excellent reasons. I simply do not accept them.'

Henry Masters reflected over his empty glass; he decided that he would go a little further. 'Nevertheless, I am not sure that the parallel is exact. The Kamblas aren't intellectual babus, nor the Comingi savages from Kiplingland. They are a race of antiquity, fairer than many of ourselves. They have an ancient culture which I for one admire. Their way of life shames us. I can think of worse fates than retiring to a Comingo village.'

'You can go there,' His Excellency said rudely.

'Why don't *you*?'

It was a shrewd blow and it halted the Governor dead. His Excellency wasn't much of a hand at touring – he preferred the Capital. He would explain, sometimes rather too carefully, that his business was the administration of the Colony, not of its Provinces. For that, though this was something he did not say, there were appropriate officials, officials who answered to himself. He had never been to the hill country.

Now he halted in mid-stride; but he recovered himself; he became in an instant the most senior official of all. Henry Masters allowed him that he did it very well. 'Yes,' he said deliberately, 'the Comingo country is something I have always wanted to see. At the moment, obviously, it is impossible.' Very carefully Sir Francis lit a cigarette. 'Which brings us back to the immediate problem. That, as I was saying, is the return of Mr Carr.'

'Quite so.'

'I should be grateful if you would see him.'

'You wouldn't prefer to see him yourself?' Masters asked. He was perfectly aware that His Excellency would not prefer to see David himself.

'I hardly think so. After all, he is not the head of Universal in the Colony. I could be kept in reserve, of course, if it became necessary. But I sincerely hope that it will not.'

'Just as you say. And what am I to tell him?'

'You are to tell him,' Sir Francis Eeles said slowly, 'that discretion is the better part of valour.'

*

At the Colony's slick new airport Carey was waiting for David Carr. David climbed from the aircraft a little stiffly. He shook hands with Carey and with the man who stood, an exact half-pace, behind him. He was a little younger than Carey and a little older than David. David knew him well, had shared a house with him for a year; but now, before Carey, they did not call each other by their Christian names. David watched this man admiringly. He was Carey's gaoler and Carey knew it. But nobody else would. He walked, like a penniless consort, slightly but just noticeably behind his master; he answered when he was spoken to, politely, a hair's-breadth short of a too obvious deference. Every senior in Universal knew that he could speak with Lord Brasted's personal authority: none would have guessed it from his manner.

The three men walked towards the airport's white buildings. Carey walked with a single hand behind his back, the palm turned outwards, holding it above the slit of his carefully countrified jacket. David didn't think he suffered from lumbago. The gesture aged him. Carey broke a silence to say: 'The Chief Secretary would like to see you, and as soon as possible.'

'Harry Masters?' David asked. He was surprised.

'Yes. There's a car, of course.'

'Then we can go together.'

But Carey hesitated. 'He didn't mention anybody else,' he said finally.

David was careful not to look at him.

Standing by the car they made their brief arrangements. David drove to the Secretariat and was shown at once to the Chief Secretary's room. Henry Masters, in his shirt-sleeves, rose to meet him. 'Take your coat off,' he said. 'Sit down.' Coatless, bow-tied, he was thin and as dry as ever, but his manner was friendly and informal. David had always liked him. A servant brought fruit drinks, something, David thought, which Carey hadn't remembered to offer.

'His Excellency asked me to have a word with you,' Masters began. 'He asked me to say that he would have liked to see you himself. . . . '

'I quite understand.'

The Chief Secretary's leathery lips opened in a surprisingly gentle smile. 'I really believe you do.'

'I think so.'

'Then we can leave the subject before either of us says anything which he might later regret. If I may I will give you His Excellency's message last. Meanwhile, if you will bear with me, I have a thought or two of my own.'

'Of course.'

Henry Masters lit David's cigarette and his own. 'You will find St Cree's changed,' he said. 'Three weeks, at the present pace, is quite a long time.'

'I can imagine it.'

'You mustn't misunderstand me. I wasn't referring to the progress of your own business, though I understand that has been considerable. I was referring to the political situation.'

David was silent and the Chief Secretary reflected. 'It's absurd,' he said to the ceiling, 'quite absurd, really. St Cree's is a dozen miles at its longest and perhaps six wide. A single man is still at large on it. There are comments which I could make, but will not, about the enthusiasm or its absence with which the hunt for him is being pressed, but the fact remains that there's the best part of a company of police on St Cree's by now. . . . And no Telemann.'

'It's an easy place to hide on,' David suggested. 'The hills . . .'

'I'm sure he's not in the Valley,' Masters said.

'So am I. But there's some pretty wild country before you reach it. Caves by the dozen, for instance.'

'Caves, as it happens, are in point. A party of police found a cave with signs of habitation. They found a radio, too. So they left a man on guard and went back to headquarters for instructions. Perfectly correct, you would think, and so would I. But when they came back with one or two more men and an officer the radio had gone and so had the guard. The guard, I needn't say, was a Kambla.'

David whistled softly.

'Precisely. It's irrelevant, I think, whether the guard's part in the affair was active or passive – whether he tipped off Telemann or one of his sympathizers, or whether he simply forgot his duty when Telemann or one of his sympathizers returned to the cave. There were no signs of a scuffle. The point is simply that Telemann *has* sympathizers. And to that a company of police isn't the answer, nor a battalion, nor a brigade for that matter.'

'Quite.'

'Even a battalion of purely Comingo police, which for the last ten years we haven't dared form. Kamblas are useless as policemen in the pinches. They're all right as bandsmen. . . .'

David smiled, remembering the Colony's Police Band. The Comingi were a musical people, but to play in a police band a Comingo considered beneath him. It wasn't at all what he had enlisted for. So the Police Band was all-Kambla. It played airs from American musicals, belting them out with a great deal of sentiment and a curiously flattened beat which turned them into a sort of nightmare plainsong.

Henry Masters's cool voice recalled him. 'So that police,' he was saying again, 'any amount of police, aren't the answer. Not formed bodies of police, that is – not official police. And the other kind we do not have.'

'We do not,' David agreed.

'I'm afraid it's inescapable that Telemann has got some way with the Kamblas on St Cree's – both the natives and the extra rough labour which the Company has had to import. He's clever and he's experienced. Disaffection is his business. He has the initiative – we are waiting his next move. I don't like that.'

David nodded and Masters changed the subject. 'We've naturally heard about that affair in London.' His tone was carefully matter-of-fact.

'Yes?'

The Chief Secretary looked directly at David. 'You are returning to considerable personal danger,' he said levelly. 'You know that, of course.'

David did not answer.

'It is my duty, and if that sounds consequential it is also to my interest, to see that reasonable precautions are taken. And I have done what I can. You will find that on the island are a handful of guards. They are armed, and I need not say that they are Comingi. They are also very discreet, not at all like those ruffians who . . . Well, we needn't go into that.' The Chief Secretary looked again at David Carr. 'I should be personally obliged if you would make the fullest use of these men. In terms, I should be grateful if you would not move abroad without one. You will find that your bungalow has already been attended to. Your European subordinates similarly.'

'But . . .'

'I put it that the request isn't unreasonable. A struggle between two states for oil is one thing – serious, granted, but it doesn't scare me personally; but when it becomes identified, personalized, if you will forgive the word, into what is evidently an organized determination to kill a particular man, yourself as it happens . . .'

David shrugged. 'Very well,' he said. 'Though I don't suppose it will make much difference.'

'Thank you nevertheless.' Henry Masters stared at the ceiling again. 'That is all I have to tell you.' He smiled ironically before he added: 'That is my message.'

'There was another, I believe,' David reminded him.

'Ah yes, there was. His Excellency charged me particularly to deliver it. I am breaking no great confidence if I tell you that His Excellency is scarcely delighted at your return.'

'And the message?' David inquired, smiling.

The Chief Secretary put the tips of his fingers together; he contrived to look pompous and very official. That, for Harry Masters, was a considerable feat. 'Discretion,' he said portentously, 'is the better part of valour. In other words, if you're going to get killed arrange it as unembarrassingly as possible.' He rose to his feet quickly. '*Au revoir*,' he said in his ordinary voice. 'Take reasonable care of yourself. And good luck, boy.'

David returned to St Cree's next morning by helicopter. That at least had been one of Carey's successes. Politely but unmistakably Head Office had told him that a new airfield was out of the question for the moment. But he had insisted on helicopters: it had been a matter of face, of personal prestige. And he had got them. There were three by now, running to a regular schedule, landing important stores and visitors of varying importance. Carey was proud of them.

David climbed from the cabin into a scene at once familiar and almost unrecognizable. In three weeks the first wave of Development had broken irresistibly. Buildings were everywhere, clean and brash and new, for there was nothing here of the charm of the older oilfields in the Colony. In the Colony were double-storeyed houses, brick and asbestos – offices and kitchens below, quarters for bachelors, refectories, above. Iron chimneys from the cooking ranges, held from the walls by six-inch clamps, climbed the sides of these houses. Their tops were splayed elaborately like a locomotive in a Railway Museum. Now, even in the oldest field, cooking was done by gas piped from the nearest source, but these chimneys still stood, undefeated and with a crazy elegance.

But on St Cree's everything was modern, everything the latest. David smiled, thinking that he would make a Preserve. He knew where it had been done, and not so far away. You found an area useless for any other purpose – a hundred yards by fifty would do. Then you built a wall, not so high that it couldn't be seen over, and you left it. You left it for ten years, twenty, fifty. The field could become a city, almost a metropolis, but between those walls was St Cree's as you had found it. David chuckled; he knew that he would be stealing an idea, but he thought it was one worth stealing.

He walked from the airstrip, passing what he realized with

a shock would soon be a chapel. Something about it struck him as incongruous. . . . Yes, the nave faced north. David's smile broadened, for he had heard of that problem too. And of its solution. You called the Bishop to consecrate your chapel and, if he protested, you talked about the Polar route, about flying the great circle, about the shortest line to Jerusalem. . . .

David had been told where it had worked. Bishops, nowadays, were exceedingly cooperative. They had to be.

Beyond the airstrip drilling had started again. It had been stopped when the big well had come in; the rigs had been dismantled, every available man put to the business of Development. But now two rigs were up again and David, joined by one of the assistants, walked to them. They were Universal's standard rig, a hundred and thirty feet from crown-block to kelly. The tables, diesel-driven, thumped noisily; the mud slipped through the screens with an air of purpose. The Comingo crews, steel-helmeted, stripped to the waist, were sweating happily. David drew a breath. The old magic was alive again.

He turned from the Comingo crews and began to walk towards the office buildings. His excitement, his pleasure began to fade, for now, mostly, they were among Kamblas. And he did not like what he observed. There was nothing, really, he told himself, nothing of open hostility or even rudeness, nothing but the unsmiling, mulish faces, too easily averted.

David sighed. He had expected nothing different, but the reality depressed him, deflated in an instant the rig's stimulus.

In the office he was brought formally up to date. Concrete had flowed with a Brazilian improvidence; the jetty, in a fortnight, would take a small tanker; piping for the well was ready, its line surveyed and a base laid. In a fortnight, in a fortnight. . . .

Nobody mentioned politics.

David walked to his bungalow, and his servant and another Comingo greeted him. The other saluted gravely. 'I am to look after you, sir,' he said; he spoke seriously, and indeed he had reason to. He had been asked to protect another man's safety, and the charge he had accepted voluntarily and for wages. If anything went wrong . . .

If anything went wrong he would certainly have to kill himself. There was nothing else for an honourable man to do.

David turned to his servant. 'Has my baggage arrived?' he asked.

'Yes, sir.'

'Then get hold of a jeep, if you would, and put it in it. I'm going to the Valley.'

The Comingo's expression was inscrutable. 'Very good, sir,' he said.

David looked at the guard. 'You had better come too.'

'But of course, sir.'

'I don't suppose I could stop you.'

The jeep arrived and David's servant put his night bag into it. 'The other thing too,' David told him.

For a moment the Comingo hesitated; then suddenly he smiled; he smiled enormously but without impertinence. '*Very* good, sir,' he said with emphasis. 'Oh, very good indeed.'

He brought the sword and put it, very carefully, beside the bag. The two Comingi, together, stepped back a pace. They stared at the sword, but they did not utter. They were gentlemen.

David spoke in Comingo. 'I can guess what you are thinking,' he said.

'It is known to me,' the guard admitted slowly, 'that Your Honour excellently understands our customs.'

'I know them a little.'

'She is very beautiful,' the butler said reflectively.

'Lovely.'

'And of the blood,' the guard added. That was important.

'As you say – of the blood.'

David knew that they were itching to see the sword, but he knew, too, that something besides good manners would restrain them. It was extremely unlucky to mention another man's weapon without his permission; to draw it would be a disaster. 'Would you care to see what I have brought for Mr Martin?' he asked.

'Your Honour is very kind,' the Comingi said together.

'Then my blessing on your hands.'

The guard took the sword and drew it slowly. 'Ah,' he said. 'Ah. . . . '

'Ah,' said the butler.

They examined the sword very carefully.

'I have never seen a better.'

'Nor one more beautiful.'

'Mr Martin is a fortunate man.'

'Doubly fortunate.'

The guard returned the sword to its scabbard and the scabbard to the jeep; he saluted again. 'A hundred sons,' he said.

'In a thousand nights,' the butler added courteously.

David and the guard climbed into the jeep.

At the bottom of the hills where the track to the Valley began its climb, a police picket stopped them. The Kambla Corporal inspected the jeep and eyed the sword; but he knew better than to touch it. He waved them forward, and David drove on, his spirits rising with the sharpening air. The guard was frowning, and David smiled, for he could guess his thoughts. He was offended; he was offended that a Kambla should bear a firearm. It had been a musket, an elderly ·303 bored for ball – not a very formidable weapon. But to a Comingo a Kambla behind gunpowder was a scandal. Not that this guard himself would be envious of firearms. David glanced at him: he hadn't even a pistol. But David knew what he had.... Not a sword, of course, but the Comingi's other speciality. At anything like close quarters it was notable enough.

For once David drove the jeep on into the Valley itself. He was aware that his visits must have excited a reasonable curiosity, and with that he was content; but he did not wish to parade a ceremonial sword before the other houses. He took the jeep to Mr Martin's, and he climbed from it and knocked. He was pleased that it was Mr Martin himself who opened.

Mr Martin greeted him with the affectionate respect which he managed so well. He began, as he always did, in English, for that was part of the pattern. 'I'm delighted to see you again,' he said. 'I hear that you have been calling while I was away.' He was looking at David very straightly.

'Yes.' David was very glad that he could meet the old man's eye.

'Please come in.'

David glanced behind him at the jeep. The guard was standing beside it; he was trying not to look too interested, but he was as alert as a terrier. David saw that he had a hand upon the sword. He turned to Mr Martin again, speaking, now, in Comingo. 'It is my wish to make you a present,' he said.

It was the proper formula.

Mr Martin looked at him again very seriously; if he was surprised he did not show it. 'Enter,' he said briefly. 'Both of you.'

They went together into the living-room. David took the sword from the guard and, bowing, taking it with both hands, held it before Mr Martin. Mr Martin took it with one. He tucked the huge sword under his right armpit – he could handle it like a walking stick – the hilt towards David.

He looked at David again and he was very solemn. Very slowly, with his left hand, he drew the blade six inches from the scabbard.

He turned to the guard. 'You shall witness,' he said.

'I shall see it.'

Jala appeared as though at a cue. She did not look at David. She walked to her father and she took the hilt. Mr Martin braced his arm and Jala shut the blade. There was a sharp click, utterly decided.

The guard struck his right hand against his left. 'It is done,' he said. 'I have seen it.'

Jala, for the first time, looked at David. She was smiling now, but still she did not come to him. Mr Martin put the sword on the table. 'I shall sleep in the schooner,' he said.

'But . . . '

'I shall sleep in the schooner.'

He kissed Jala and shook hands with David. He was smiling now, enormous, fatherly. 'Be happy,' he said. 'Be fruitful.'

He was gone.

The guard stood in the corner, grinning contentedly. 'The moon is so full,' he said. It was broad daylight, but that was how you took leave of a wedding.

'The stars cannot match the moon.'

The guard, too, disappeared.

Jala was in his arms and David began to kiss her in a crescendo which, in a moment, was unconscious. She dropped her head upon his shoulder, shivering. 'Now,' she said, almost sleepily. 'Now and now.'

David, very early, pinched Jala awake. She moved against him at once, sighing, expectant. Presently David said: 'I've forgotten something.'

Jala giggled. 'Then God help me,' she said impiously.

David laughed. 'I didn't mean quite that.' He put on his

dressing gown, crossing to the coat which he had hung across a chair. He didn't remember doing so. He took something from the pocket; he had bought it at the shop to which he had directed his taxi after the swordsmith's. It had cost even more than the sword. It wasn't a ring, for the Comingi would not wear them. Rings were a symbol of eternity, and to the Comingi eternity was an idea without meaning.

He returned to Jala, the case in his hand. 'Sit up,' he said.

Jala seemed to hesitate. 'Like this?' she inquired.

'Like that.'

David put the pearls round her neck. She fingered them, searching him with an expression which he could not read; she began to cry quietly.

'What in the world's the matter?'

Jala did not answer; she pulled him down beside her again, half laughing. She was absurdly happy, so she began to cry again.

David would not let Jala return with him. He took the jeep and the guard, sobering by now from the party which Mr Martin had floated before he left. It had been a very good party indeed. They drove down the track and, at the police post, another vehicle was on the point of starting its climb. In it were another guard and one of David's assistants. He was evidently worried. 'You'd better be quick,' he said briefly.

'Why?'

'The Kamblas are at your bungalow. Every man jack of them.'

'What for?'

'They won't say, and they won't go away either. They say they want you personally.'

David grunted.

The two cars drove to the bungalow and David walked through it to the veranda. He was perfectly collected – this wasn't his first brush with Kamblas. He saw at once that his assistant hadn't greatly exaggerated. The Kamblas were sitting in an immense crescent, their chattering dying into silence as he appeared. One man rose from the centre of the foremost rank. David knew him. His name was Bosoli. He was a clerk, Company-educated, one of the very few Kamblas to rise above menial labour. He was a little less dirty than most and his clothes were European, but, inescapably, he was still a Kambla. The silent throng rose as he did, shuffling behind him as he approached the veranda. They didn't intend to miss anything. They squatted again as David sat on the veranda step. Bosoli stayed standing. He took off his terrible hat, smiling toothily. There was something sebaceous about him.

'Who sent you?' David asked.

'Nobody sent us.' Bosoli dropped his eyes. 'We came,' he said.

David did not press him; he had made him lie, and he was aware that Bosoli knew it. That, for the moment, was enough.

'What can I do for you?'

Bosoli began. It was at once evident that he had prepared a considerable speech, and David knew better than to interrupt him. It would have been very bad manners to try, and quite useless. Bosoli began with a good deal of flattery. The Kamblas, he said, in English of a sort, were a poor and an oppressed people; they had enemies even in their own country, a race which had arrived from no one knew where. Kamblas were misunderstood, despised for their poverty, held in contempt for reasons which were themselves contemptible. They were friendless. . . . Well, almost. For every now and then, once in a generation, God sent them a Good Man. A friend. A man wise and noble – above the stupid prejudices of others. A man to trust. A David Carr, in fact.

David listened politely. He was thirsty and would have given a good deal for a cup of tea. But it would have been exceedingly rude to have sent for one. To smoke, too, would also have been unseemly.

'I will help you if I can,' he said simply. He spoke in Kambla.

There was a murmur from the squatting mass, but Bosoli hadn't finished his preamble. He moved to its second leg, which was something to do with the rights of Man. David heard him out in a sort of dream. There were the City States of Greece and Thomas Paine and President Wilson – all the ragbag of an education half-comprehended. David hadn't an idea what it was leading to: it might be another twopence an hour or it might only be the tea in the canteen.

But Bosoli, at last, was working towards his peroration. 'So,' he was saying, 'we are asking no more than is our due, we are demanding no more than our natural, our inalienable rights. We are men, sir, as you are. We are men, made in the image of God.' He raised his arms and let them fall again. It would have been impressive if it hadn't been ludicrous.

'Thank you,' David said.

Bosoli, too, sat down. The speech was over, hard bargaining now in order.

'What do you want?' David asked. Half an hour earlier the question would have been an insult.

'Sir,' Bosoli said, 'sir, we want a plebiscite.'

'A plebiscite?' David echoed involuntarily. He was utterly astonished.

'A plebiscite, sir.'

'What on earth are you going to do with it?'

'We are going to decide our future,' Bosoli said.

He had it very pat.

David thought quickly. This wasn't Kambla form at all, nor even Bosoli's. Bosoli had been briefed. Very competently. To gain time he asked slowly: 'Do you think you could run the island on your own?'

'I think so, sir.'

‘And what, for instance, would you use for food?’

‘We should manage.’

‘You said you trusted me, and I will tell you the truth. I don’t think you *could* manage. Not you, the Kamblas of St Cree’s, nor anybody else. I don’t think anybody could run this island independently of some other country.’

Bosoli dropped his eyes again, shuffling his feet. Under David’s inspection, cool and unhostile, he writhed visibly. It was evident that he did not wish to speak but that he would. ‘We might not have to,’ he said at last.

So that was it! Laramonda . . .

David rose at once and Bosoli with him. David looked at the crowd of Kamblas. ‘What is the Kambla for “plebiscite”?’ he asked.

‘I – I don’t know. I don’t think . . . Sir, please . . .’

David smiled. ‘Do your friends understand what you are asking me?’ he inquired.

‘No – not properly. They are ignorant men, sir.’

‘Be silent.’ David considered for some time. ‘I am going to say something to your friends,’ he said finally, ‘and in Kambla. What would you like me to say?’

‘Sir, I am in your hands.’

‘As it happens I believe you are. It doesn’t advance me, though, to destroy you.’

‘Oh sir . . . Please . . . Say, then, that you will forward what I have asked. To the authorities. To the proper authorities.’

It was an abracadabra.

‘Very well.’ David raised his head to the Kamblas, speaking over Bosoli’s. ‘I have heard,’ he said, ‘and what has been asked was never mine to give. But I will send it before the High One.’ He raised his hand in dismissal. ‘Peace be on you.’

‘Peace,’ the Kamblas answered in ragged chorus. They did not seem too disappointed.

David turned to Bosoli again. He wasn't angry – he was almost sorry for him. 'Good evening,' he said in English. 'I will tell my superior.' He smiled almost kindly. 'No doubt you will do the same.'

Chapter Eight

Edward Carr was calling on Lord Brasted by invitation. It was half past six and Brasted was opening a bottle of champagne. He detested mixed drinks and would decline a cocktail in a palace. But champagne was one of his specialities and, like his eyeglass, it wasn't an affectation. He liked champagne; he understood it. He opened a bottle at half past six every evening of his life. If he were going out later his taste was well enough known, he was more than sufficiently eminent, for it to be indulged by whoever was his host. And if he wasn't going out he sat at home and finished his own bottle.

Now he crossed to the sideboard and twisted the wire with strong fingers; he pressed against the cork with his thumbs and it slipped from the bottle with barely a sound. The bottle was held properly – nothing escaped. No fuss, Carr reflected, no tiresome bang, no splashing. Brasted was used to champagne. It will be one of half a dozen, the Minister decided, and one, incomprehensibly popular, it certainly will not – not the Racecourse Brand, not the Bookies' Special. It was extraordinary how that label had been built up – advertising, he supposed, and plain snobbery. Here today, for in the *demimonde* you were considered unfashionable if you asked for any other; and gone tomorrow; gone in favour of the next importer who thought the cost of advertising worth the candle. Lord Brasted raised his glass and Edward Carr his.

No, it certainly wasn't the Bookies' Special. It was admirable. He was inclined to think it was a Krug.

They sat in comfortable arm-chairs by the fireside. Presently Lord Brasted said: 'It's clever all right.'

The Minister knew what he was referring to. 'This business of a plebiscite,' he said thoughtfully. 'Yes, it's a clever move – unexpected as well.'

'A plebiscite. . . . ' Brasted rolled the word round his tongue with his wine. 'It doesn't *mean* anything,' he announced. 'It's an incantation, a sort of spell. *Om Mani Padme Hum.* Oh, Flower of the Lotus! Oh, Plebiscite! Oh, flower of every knock-kneed European constitution of the Twenties.'

'Exactly.'

'But spells summon spirits – sometimes inconvenient ones. May I ask your reactions to plebiscite if I were to intone it appropriately and for long enough?'

Edward Carr smiled. 'If you were a rather old-fashioned psychiatrist and I on your couch I should answer to plebiscite quickly enough. I should say men in duffle coats and dingy beards. I should say women with unpublished novels. I should say dons with political ambitions and painters who couldn't sell their pictures nor design a decent book-cover for bread and butter.'

'And if I were the old-fashioned psychiatrist, and honest, I should pocket your guineas and discharge you as indecently normal.'

Lord Brasted poured more wine. 'Those people,' he said a little vaguely, sipping his champagne. 'Do they trouble you?'

'Politically, you mean?'

Lord Brasted nodded and the Secretary of State reflected. 'Yes and no,' he said at length. 'By the final test of politics, by the test of the ballot-box, they are inconsiderable. They congregate in perhaps a couple of dozen constituencies, and even there they don't call the tune. I'd rather annoy them than the smallest Union. But it's undeniable that they're vocal. They can make a disproportionate noise.'

'And noise', Lord Brasted suggested, 'is precisely what, at the moment, you least fancy?'

'It is.'

'An international noise particularly?'

'Quite so.'

It was Brasted's turn to consider, and when he spoke again he seemed to have changed the subject. 'We seem to be meeting Clementi's moves as he makes them,' he said, 'or trying to.'

'I'm afraid we do.'

'It would help if you could give me some idea of the limits upon your own action. Naturally I do not ask for confidences, but if you could give me an inkling of the political coordinates. . . . '

'I don't mind telling you how I saw it before this plebiscite business came along.'

'It would be very helpful.'

The Secretary of State spread his hands. 'On your own head be it.' He accepted another glass of champagne. 'Like yourself,' he went on, 'I had rather conceded that Clementi held the political initiative as I am advised that he undoubtedly holds the military. But I had also assumed that he didn't want war, or at least that he didn't want war if he could gain his object by other means. That object is obviously possession of St Cree's, which in present circumstances is simply possession of this oil. So that in the game of poker which resulted I knew or could reasonably guess one thing about Clementi's hand: he would use all means short of war but not war itself, not in the sense of starting one deliberately, for I argued that with military superiority, at least locally, he would have started one already if he had meant to. But if I knew, or thought I knew one limitation on Clementi's hand I also reckoned that he knew none on mine. He could estimate, for instance, the penalties I should risk if I put troops on to St Cree's. But he didn't *know*. My one advantage was that he simply didn't know how far I would go.'

Lord Brasted nodded. 'Very lucid,' he said. 'And how far will you?'

The Minister grimaced. 'Is that what you mean by political coordinates?' he inquired.

'I think so.'

'I told you before that the political situation domestically was rather nicely balanced.'

'You did. And may I remind you that I told you in turn that if we went ahead with collecting this oil for you we should be entitled to protection.'

Edward Carr smiled again. 'You also told me that if anything went wrong politically you reserved the right to make my life a misery.'

'Very possibly,' Lord Brasted said blandly.

'James, are you putting the finger on me?'

Brasted's expression did not change. 'If you must put it so crudely,' he admitted.

'It won't get you anywhere, you know.'

Lord Brasted thought for a long time. Finally he said slowly: 'I think you are right. I could perhaps oblige you to do something which you did not wish to, but I cannot compel you to do something which may be outside your authority.... Is that what you're telling me?'

'More or less.'

'Then we are still allies.'

The Minister held up his hand. 'You must not ask me to define our enemies,' he said.

'I wouldn't dream of it.'

'Though I do not mind admitting that some of my colleagues have uncomfortably thin skins. They were sensitive a week or two ago, and now that we are refusing a plebiscite, now that we are illiberal Imperialists, all of us . . . '

Lord Brasted said something about illiberal Imperialists.

'Quite. But in this at least we are together, for a plebiscite on St Cree's is an evident nonsense. That is something, I think.'

'You had better stay that way,' Lord Brasted said simply, 'if you want this oil.'

'I needn't say that I agree.'

Lord Brasted thought again. 'It is curious,' he went on after a little, 'what oil can do to people. Legacies and oil and women. . . . You think you have them and suddenly you haven't – the other fellow looks like getting them instead. . . . Things begin to happen even to the most high-principled person. Things begin to occur. . . . '

'I hope you're right.'

'Experience suggests I am.' Lord Brasted spoke a little grimly, fetching the bottle again. 'Let me know if I can help.'

'Thank you – I certainly will.' Edward Carr raised his replenished glass. 'There's one thing here and now,' he said, 'not political, but David. . . . '

'David will be all right.'

'I wish I were as confident.'

'If you're thinking of his physical safety then you no doubt know that Masters has arranged certain precautions. And for your own ear alone my Company has added one or two of its own. We have had to be discreet about it, of course – your brother isn't the man to relish strutting about with a bodyguard. But in fact he is rather more carefully looked after than he knows. Short of a rifle shot in the back . . . '

'That's what I'm afraid of.'

Lord Brasted did not answer. David had told him something of Telemann; he had been fascinated, he couldn't be sure, but . . .

But certainly that wasn't a subject for the Secretary of State.

'But personal safety apart,' the Minister was saying, 'David must expect a great deal more trouble.'

'How do you see the affair developing?' Brasted asked.

'I should guess that the next move would be a strike.'

'Which I shouldn't particularly mind.'

'What was that?' Edward Carr asked sharply. He was astonished and sounded it.

'We shouldn't particularly mind a strike,' Lord Brasted repeated coolly, 'for it would be mistimed. More precisely, the moment for it has passed. Most of the heavy work on St Cree's is done. We had plans, naturally, for treating these Kamblas decently. The extra labour which we brought in was mostly in our employment already: we should simply have sent it back to the Colony. And for most of the Kamblas native to the island we could have found something – care and maintenance and so on. For most but not all – that is the point. A month ago when we wanted any labour we could persuade to work for us – any hand that could turn a shovel – a month ago a strike would have been a serious embarrassment. But today ...' Lord Brasted shrugged. 'Today,' he concluded, 'we could survive.'

'It would be hell for me, though,' the Minister said.

'I can see that.'

'Putting troops on to an island where there happened to be a strike would be as explosive domestically as putting troops on to a demilitarized island would be dangerous internationally.'

'I could myself write the speeches about it,' Lord Brasted said dryly.

'I should be a Fascist Beast, I should be Black, a Scab, a ...'

'Indubitably you would.' Lord Brasted chuckled unexpectedly. 'Is this another limitation on your freedom of action?'

'I'm afraid it is.'

'As no doubt are the political connexions of those thugs who attacked your brother?'

Edward Carr nodded.

'That is known, I suppose – where it matters, I mean? I know and you know, and so far the Press, thank heaven, doesn't. But your colleagues . . . ?'

'The information didn't go only to myself.'

'And your colleagues, the ones you were mentioning, the gentlemen with uncomfortably thin skins?'

The Secretary of State smiled dourly; he became noticeably Scots. 'Thin skins,' he said, 'don't invariably go with weak hearts, one isn't exactly a symptom of the other, but . . . '

'God help us all,' Lord Brasted said. He sounded philosophical rather than depressed. He rang the bell and a servant brought another bottle.

*

The Kambla who appeared that evening at the bottom of the veranda steps was as ragged and dirty as the next, but something about him at once caught David's attention. For one thing he was surprised to see him there at all. There was a fence round the bungalow now and, though it wasn't impenetrable, David suspected that it was discreetly patrolled; and for another this Kambla was astonishingly well made. Under his rags he was stocky and powerful. He smiled unexpectedly, making a gesture which in an instant betrayed him; he bowed a little stiffly. 'I am unarmed,' he said.

It didn't occur to David to disbelieve him; he went down the steps and stood before Telemann. 'I can hardly ask you in.'

Telemann bowed again. 'Perfectly,' he said.

David considered him. At last he said: 'You will forgive me, but you spoke once before about bravado. . . . '

Telemann shrugged. 'I know I did. I repeat that it is a

weakness – a weakness of my race. It unfits us, really, for the career which I have embraced. As do one or two other characteristics, for that matter. But it isn't bravado tonight.'

'Why have you come, then?'

'To apologize,' Telemann said simply.

David did not smile. 'You mean that affair in London?' he asked. 'But I did not imagine that it was your personal contrivance.'

'It was a disgrace. Three to one, an unarmed man . . . '

'It hadn't the Telemann touch,' David said coolly.

'I am delighted that you agree.'

David looked at Telemann again. 'You're a very strange man,' he said.

'I'm afraid I'm a very inefficient one. In my youth I was subjected to a certain conditioning. I was a Catholic, for instance. That I can truthfully say I have sloughed, for to do so was an intellectual exercise, but I must confess that I have found it much harder to escape from the prejudices of my class.'

'Class,' David echoed in astonishment.

Telemann smiled. 'It's almost a dirty word nowadays, isn't it?' he asked. 'Like – like ineluctable.'

It was David's turn to smile. 'Like ineluctable,' he admitted.

'But a great deal more precise, and a great deal more valid. I – I whom they sometimes hamstring – I assure you that the habits, the prejudices of class are almost inescapable.' Telemann stared levelly at David. 'You should know that too,' he added. 'You're no better than I am.'

'If you're the man you may be I'm certainly not.'

Telemann waved this aside. 'I wasn't speaking socially,' he said, 'for I am not a boor. I was being entirely practical.'

'I'm not sure that I follow you.'

'When I said I was unarmed you believed me, didn't you?'

'I suppose I did.'

'You should consider that, my friend.'

'I will,' David said thoughtfully.

'And you had a firearm somewhere within a few paces?'

'I did.'

'So that you could have taken it and shot me. You could have shot me dead, or wounded and taken me. There would have been a dozen excuses.'

'I suppose so,' David said again.

'But you did not.'

'Evidently.'

Telemann smiled again. 'I have made my point, I think. It would have been sensible to shoot me – in a sense it was your duty to. You failed, you know, as I have failed. . . . And am failing.'

David was silent.

'I am trying to tell you that I understand,' Telemann added presently. 'I am happy to have apologized for that affair in London, but happier that you agree that it was no planning of mine. Not that that makes the least difference, of course. I realize that: that is what I am trying to say. I wasn't responsible but *we* were.' Telemann made his little bow again. 'I came to tell you,' he said formally, 'that I will give you the opportunity. I have never refused an equal.'

'Thank you,' David heard himself saying.

'And now, if you will excuse me, I will go.'

'I will come with you.'

They walked up the drive of the bungalow to the gate in the fence. An astonished policeman saluted. 'This man has been to see me,' David said. 'Pass him.'

'But Your Honour, he did not come by me. I did not see . . .'

'You did not see him,' David said, 'and now you do not see.' He turned to Telemann. 'Good night.'

'Good night.'

David, a little surprised, discovered that he was returning Telemann's bow.

He walked back to the bungalow reflectively. 'It is a weakness of my race,' he thought. What race? Telemann's English was almost perfect. David was certain he had met him; his name was on the tip of his tongue....

David returned next evening from his office to the bungalow. He entered from the back, across the compound which separated the two buildings, and his servant met him on the back veranda. 'They are here again,' he said.

The Comingi had four words for They: there was They ceremonial, They ordinary, They domestic, and They contemptuous. The butler had used the fourth and David at once knew whom he meant. He glanced through the living-room and the front veranda. The Kamblas had gathered again, Bosoli in the front rank. 'I don't think they've seen me yet,' David said. 'Bring me a drink, please.'

His servant brought a chair and a whisky and soda, and David drank reflectively. He wasn't greatly disturbed; he could guess the object of this visitation and he hoped that he could handle it. He allowed himself a second whisky and a cigarette. When he had finished them he rose and walked to the front of the bungalow.

Bosoli got up at once. As he had done before he took six steps towards David, and the Kamblas shuffled behind him. There seemed to be a few more than there had been. They squatted again as David sat. This time he did not sit on the veranda steps – he signed to his servant for a chair. Little things like that were important; they could set the climate of a discussion, make it or wreck it. Bosoli remained standing.

'I gave your message,' David said, 'as I agreed to. You will have heard the answer.'

The Resident Magistrate had in fact given it. He had convened a public meeting, and had regretted, politely but quite firmly, that though the proposal for a plebiscite upon St

Cree's had been given the most careful consideration, not only by Her Majesty's representative in the Colony but also by Her Majesty's Government – though the fullest and most careful consideration had been given to the suggestion, he was instructed to say that the proposal appeared to be premature. At the same time the suggestion would of course always be borne in mind, and in the light of developing circumstances . . .

It had all been very correct.

Bosoli had been at the meeting, and evidently his prestige hadn't increased by it. David knew that he was a figurehead, that his position rested on nothing more solid than a clerical job and a smattering of English; he knew, too, that prestige was a slippery, a tenuous thing: it grew or it diminished, it never stood still and, once lost, it was terribly difficult to recover. David had been expecting some move from Bosoli, and here it was.

Bosoli's manner had subtly altered. It certainly wasn't assured – it was impossible to imagine Bosoli sure of himself – but there was something about it which David found it difficult to define. There was something febrile, almost a desperation.

'We have heard the answer,' he was saying, 'and we do not accept it.'

David shrugged. 'I can do no more myself.'

'But you must.'

'Little man,' David reflected, ' "must" is not a word. . . . ' But he kept his temper; he was thinking that between Prelate and Sovereign 'must', whatever it wasn't, was at least a word commonly apprehended. It was a term of art. Whereas with Bosoli, wretched bumbling Bosoli . . .

'Why must I?' David asked. His tone was still carefully courteous. 'Who says I must?'

'We say so. We, the people of St Cree's.'

David, now, lit a cigarette, conscious that the gesture

wouldn't be wasted. 'What gave you the idea?' he inquired. He wouldn't, just yet, say Who?

Bosoli's voice changed slightly. 'Sir,' he said for the first time, 'sir, we wish to be free, to decide our destiny. We are men, sir, we have rights, the rights of humanity. . . .'

'I know – you told me. But what made you think of them – now, I mean?'

Bosoli dropped his eyes and David leant forward in his chair. 'Who put you up to this?' he asked now. He didn't raise his voice.

'Nobody,' Bosoli said finally.

'Nobody?'

Bosoli was silent.

David sat on, alert and aware, sensing the assembled Kamblas. They didn't understand English, but they had an animal's instinct for tones and voices. Something was happening to them, something he couldn't put his finger on. At last he said slowly: 'So what happens now?'

He realized at once that he had made a mistake. Bosoli had an opening and he took it. 'Then since you will not help us,' he said, 'we must help ourselves.'

'How?' David inquired. He saw that he was committed.

'We shall strike,' Bosoli said.

'For a plebiscite?'

'For our rights.'

David considered; he noticed that the Kamblas, sliding on their bottoms, had edged a little nearer. 'Your people are with you in this?' he asked.

'Of course. To a man.'

'You have told them that the work on St Cree's – their work – is almost done? That in a week or so we could dispense with them? If we were obliged to, that is. It hadn't been our intention to do so.'

'Yes,' Bosoli said. But he had fatally hesitated.

'Do you object if I tell them too? In Kambla?'

'Sir,' Bosoli began, 'Your Honour. . . .'

But David had come to an immediate decision. He rose, towering above Bosoli on the veranda steps; he repeated in Kambla what he had just told Bosoli.

There was a moment of silence whilst the words sunk in. Then, quite deliberately, the Kamblas rose; they surrounded Bosoli; they began to chatter, loudly, excitedly. David mightn't have been there.

He slipped into the bungalow and found his servant. 'You'd better get the police,' he said. 'And hurry.' He spoke with reluctance, unwilling to admit a failure. But he gave the order.

The Comingo butler glanced at what was by now the mob, grasping the situation in an instant, disappearing at the double.

Outside the voice of the Kamblas had deepened. Across it cut shrilly Bosoli's protests. The mutter of the mob rose suddenly that final, that terrifying half-tone. David heard a single scream, appalled and appalling.

Two policemen came running from the gate, their muskets at the ready. But they were much too late. The wave of Kamblas broke over them, two pebbles on an open beach, streaming down the drive, silently now, cattle in stampede, as unreasoning and as dangerous.

David went down from the veranda, looking at what was left of Bosoli. He walked to the bungalow again, putting one hand against the wall. He was horribly, comprehensively sick.

David did not go to bed that night, for he did not dare. He knew the Kamblas and he knew what they would do. Up to a point. They wouldn't proceed at once to riot and ruin; instead they would first go home. David knew what they would do there, what in fact they would be doing at this moment. They would be drinking. They weren't supposed to have alcohol, the Company did everything possible to keep it from them, but somehow they always possessed it – a terrifying, a barbarous brew. Blood, David reflected, the sight and smell of blood, and this murderous toddy. He shrugged. There wasn't a thing he could do about it – nothing effective. He could alert the police and he had done so. He could telephone to the mainland. But at bottom he couldn't influence the matter. The Kamblas might sit at home, boozing themselves into a bestial stupor. In which case the Company would lose a day's work from them next day. Or the drink might explode in them, suddenly, incalculably. . . .

In which case the Company stood to lose something more substantial than a mere day's work.

David shrugged again. It was a toss-up and he knew it.

He was dozing in his chair when his servant woke him. The Comingo was wearing his own clothes, his dagger in his belt. With him was the night guard and David's two assistants. They were strained and white. It was midnight and moonless, but, in the glow of the fires outside, the room was almost light. 'The well,' David began.

'They haven't touched it yet,' the senior assistant told him. 'It's some way off. . . . Perhaps . . .'

'What about the Magistrate?'

'He's down on the jetty. There was nothing he could do. There's a launch if he needs it. He's all right, I think. Actually they don't seem much interested in any of us.'

'And the police?' David asked.

'They're doing what they can, or some of them are. I didn't see many, though. It was all very sudden. . . . '

'It would be. . . . No firing?'

'Not yet.'

'And the Comingi?'

'They've kept their heads, thank God. They've gone to the power station; they're behind the wire. Most of them, I should say, and the families too.'

'We'd better have a look,' David said resignedly. 'I don't

suppose we can do much, but we ought to make sure that nobody shoots. The first Comingo policeman to pull a trigger . . .'

'They know it,' the assistant said.

The little party walked from the bungalow into a nightmare. It was a scene by Bruegel the Elder, its background pointed not by snow and ice, not by the lances of Alba's horsemen, but by the flames which rose from the blazing buildings. But the Kamblas were the authentic grotesques. Knots of them formed suddenly; broke inexplicably; lurched into outer darkness singing obscenely. Some had burning torches, some fed the flames with whatever they could lay hands on. In their insensate way they had made a very good job of it. St Cree's was ablaze.

'We'll go to the power station,' David said.

Here was another world, a world of calm and sanity. The Comingi, tightly packed, sat in the wired compound. Normally a Comingo would conceal his weapon, but tonight the men, like David's servant, had their knives in their sashes. Here and there a child cried fretfully, but the women were entirely peaceful. They knew that they would not die before their men, and if their men died first they would not wish to live.

A tall old man, his beard a rival to Mr Martin's, came to meet them. David recognized him. He was the senior Comingo on the island, not the Company's senior Comingo employee. He was of the blood, and David smiled at him; he was thinking that the Comingi in a crisis had never lacked leaders. Now they were much too wise to have considered a Company's hierarchy; they had a headman here, a nobleman.

David shook hands. 'You have done well. I am grateful to you.'

'Your Honour is very kind.'

'I am sorry this has happened.'

The Comingo shrugged. 'It came very suddenly,' he said. 'These animals . . .'

'And what will happen now, do you think?'

'The drink will die in them,' the Comingo said, 'but not before morning. Not before our work is destroyed.'

'And the well?' David asked.

The headman smiled. 'They will not think of it,' he said. 'They do not think,' he added grimly.

'I hope you're right.'

'Do not try and guard it, though. Do not remind them.'

David hesitated, for the decision was difficult. He looked at the old Comingo, wise and serene. 'Very well,' he said finally.

'As Your Honour has decided,' the Comingo said politely. David turned to the crowded compound. 'You have everything you need?' he asked.

'We have water and a little food for the children – enough until tomorrow. Tomorrow there will be peace. Of a sort.'

'I hope you are right,' David said again.

'Tomorrow they will lie like the dogs they are.'

'In the ashes,' David said unhappily.

The headman, for once, had no answer; courteously he withdrew his gaze.

'God with you.'

'And with Your Honour.'

The five men walked back to the bungalow. Such police as were visible had ringed it, and a native officer met them. He was another Comingo, worried but not afraid. 'I hope I have done what you would wish,' he said.

'You have done excellently. Not a shot . . . ?'

'Not a shot, Your Honour. We were tempted, though.'

'You have done well,' David repeated.

Across the compound the roof of the office building fell in a flaming crash.

The telephone rang peremptorily. 'They haven't remembered to cut it,' one of the assistants said. He hadn't much experience of Kamblas and he was astonished.

David took the telephone. For a moment it buzzed angrily before Carey came through. 'Carr?' he inquired. 'Carr?' He was evidently in a tizzy.

'Speaking.'

'You're all right then? Thank God. What the devil's going on?'

'How do you know about it?'

'The Magistrate got through to us. Where have you been? We've been trying to get you.'

'I've been looking around,' David said.

'But damn it . . . '

'What did that beak tell you?'

'He said the place was in flames; he said there was a riot.'

'He exaggerated.'

'But everything is on fire, isn't it?'

'Most of it,' David admitted. 'Not the well, though.'

'And the Kamblas . . . ?'

'Will be sober tomorrow.'

'You must return at once,' Carey said.

'What was that?'

'You must come back at once. Take the launch. Bring the assistants, and the Magistrate if you can find him. We can sort it out later, send the soldiers perhaps. . . . '

'I shall do no such thing.' The assistants behind David murmured an assent. They hadn't heard the whole of the conversation, but they were conscious that Carey was giving an instruction which David Carr didn't fancy.

They were with David.

'But damn it, man . . . '

David lost his temper. 'Don't "man" me, blast you,' he said furiously; he drew a considerable breath. 'What do you think we are? There are five hundred Comingi on this island. We employ them. Do you think I'm going to run like a rat?

Do you think I could speak to a Comingo again? Do you think the others would come with me if I told them to? What the devil do you take us for?'

'Don't talk to me like that.'

'I shall talk as I please. You're all right for having people beaten up, all right as long as you're not there. . . . Now you expect me to run.'

'Don't be a perfect bloody fool. You're not some two-and-a-half-striper going down in a destroyer and a blaze of glory. I don't like heroics.'

'And I,' David said acidly, 'don't like cowards.'

'Damn your eyes for an impertinent boy.' There was a moment of silence. 'Well, those are my orders,' Carey said finally.

'Yours?' David inquired.

Carey knew what he meant. 'Mine,' he said, choking.

'To the devil with your orders.'

'You're not coming?'

'I'm coming all right. When it suits me. When I think it's proper to.' David drew another breath. 'And when I do,' he said calmly, 'I shall bring my wife with me.' He smiled; he was cool again now. 'Put that in your silly pipe and smoke it if you can.'

Chapter Nine

Edward Carr was sitting in his room waiting to attend the Cabinet Meeting which had been called at eleven. He was smiling and in excellent heart, for he was getting the breaks and he knew it. A riot on St Cree's, he thought – it had changed everything. For into his meadow had walked the most sacred of all the Sacred Cows. She was called the Queen's Peace, or sometimes the Duty to Preserve It, and at a swish of her venerable tail the flies had risen respectfully. The Queen's Peace – it simplified superbly; it was an Issue, clear-cut and unequivocal; it couldn't be ignored and, inescapably, it had to be decided.

The Minister chuckled contentedly, for he was reasonably sure what the decision would be. Nevertheless he was a careful man; he knew that he had colleagues who would resent the necessity to commit themselves, colleagues who would writhe upon the pin. But he had done rather more than passively accept good fortune: he had had a word with the Rabbit.

He walked briskly up Whitehall, still smiling, swinging his umbrella, thinking that his Cabinet arithmetic had been both right and wrong. The Cabinet didn't vote. You couldn't, when constitutionally you accepted collective responsibility, formally go on record against a policy unless you were prepared to resign on it. As you almost certainly were not. So you didn't formally vote. Any textbook would tell you that, and it would be quite right. Also more than a little misleading, since in a perfectly intelligible sense the Cabinet *did* vote; the Sense of the Meeting emerged with less bother and a good deal more clearly than sometimes happened in the Euston Road, and it was curious, the Minister reflected, how regularly that sense was proportional to the arithmetical majority in the inner ring. Edward Carr smiled again, a little dourly now, for it had struck him that his reflections were scarcely English. Well, he wasn't an Englishman. Nevertheless it was something more than a coincidence. There were six or seven in the inner ring, and somehow, if they broke five to two, whoever was taking the full Cabinet Minute would find himself with something which looked like a five to two decision. The Minute wouldn't say so, of course – perish the thought. But that is how the sense it recorded would read.

And the Rabbit was in the inner ring and Edward Carr had been to see him. He was a peer, and the reason for his nickname declared itself the instant he opened his mouth. Which he made a point of doing as seldom as he could. He was a taciturn man, shrewd and of a vast experience. More important to Edward Carr he was the keeper of the party's conscience. The Duty to Preserve the Peace. . . . He had listened to the Secretary of State with care, showing his appalling fangs infrequently, asking an occasional question. He hadn't promised support but he had inferred it. Edward Carr was confident.

He walked into the too-carefully preserved Victoriana of the Cabinet Room, realizing that he was almost the first to arrive, noticing that the Secretary himself wasn't there. Somebody explained that he was sick. One of his juniors was fussing with pencils and a notebook, very keen, efficient too obviously. He was a clever official but an unhappy man; he hadn't always been in the Administrative Grade and he was conscious of it. Now that he had arrived, had joined a club, had letters after his name – now an early and inconvenient marriage gnawed him unmercifully. He was stout and a little pompous and very good at his job.

The room filled quickly, for they were busy men and punctual. Presently the Prime Minister sat down and the others after him. Edward Carr managed a good look at him without staring; he thought he looked extremely fit. He knew he had returned from abroad that morning, for it was a convention by now that the Prime Minister should be the Representative, the Great Traveller, the bearer of strange devices into pleasant little towns in professionally neutral states which made an excellent living out of housing conferences. That didn't detract from his skill upon the high wire of domestic politics. No travels impaired his superbly competent management. He was naturally a very good chairman.

Now he tapped on the table, looking at Edward Carr. 'St Cree's,' he said briefly.

The meeting was a regular one, but the subject had been put into the agenda as a matter of urgency. There wasn't a paper on it, and Edward Carr shortly recited its history. He did it well, impersonally and without comment. He was good at explanation.

'I see,' the Prime Minister said. Edward Carr braced himself for the questioning he expected, but it was clear that the Prime Minister wasn't in the mood for extended debate; he turned at once to Her Majesty's Principal Secretary of State for Foreign Affairs. 'Well?' he inquired.

'It is a most awkward situation,' the Foreign Secretary said, 'most complicated and dangerous.'

Something happened to the Prime Minister's eyebrows. They didn't exactly rise in surprise, nor could you say that he had frowned in irritation. The Prime Minister was never irritated, or if he was he never showed it. He could not afford to. It was an expression which only the perfect chairman could have contrived. 'I agree,' he said smoothly. 'But I was asking for your reactions.'

'It is an evident risk that any overt action on St Cree's will provoke Clementi.'

'Agreed again.'

'And we know from events as they have occurred that a certain Power must be willing to back him.'

'It is a fair assumption generally, though I'm not convinced that the event to which I take it you refer necessarily reinforces it. One scoundrel will often help another in what is after all a detail. I'm not sure I would accept that affair as evidence that Clementi's ally has committed himself in general. Finally. To the point of war, for example.'

The Foreign Secretary was silent.

'That is the crux,' somebody said.

'I am glad you agree.' The Prime Minister looked again at Edward Carr. 'If I do not canvass your own opinion,' he said, 'it is because I am taking it as known. In your own Office I should have no doubt about my duty.'

'Thank you, Prime Minister.'

'It is the international repercussions which we have to consider.' The Prime Minister turned once more to the Foreign Secretary. 'Well?' he asked again.

'We seem to be agreed that a risk of war exists.'

'We are.' The Prime Minister's expression sharpened almost imperceptibly. 'But Laramonda is not the only state with an ally. You have sounded our own, no doubt.'

'Recently, you mean? On this issue specifically? I'm afraid not yet. I . . .'

'That should have been done,' the Prime Minister said.

There was a murmur round the table. Edward Carr judged that rather more men had uttered than had kept silent.

The Prime Minister was still looking at the Foreign Secretary. It was common knowledge that he didn't particularly like him, and evidently he didn't intend to let him off lightly. 'So you haven't been to our ally,' he went on reflectively. He seemed to be speaking to himself.

'But I have,' the Rabbit said surprisingly. He held up his hand as Her Majesty's Principal Secretary of State for Foreign Affairs began to bristle. 'Naturally it was quite informal, and in fact quite accidental. I met their Ambassador last night – at dinner. As it happens it was he who made the approaches.'

'What did he say?'

'He said that Mr President would be very unhappy to see St Cree's in any hands but our own.'

'Of course he did.'

'So,' the Rabbit continued calmly, 'so I felt entitled to ask him what would be Mr President's reactions if that looked like happening and we were obliged to take steps to prevent it. . . . And got ourselves into trouble in the process.'

'And what did he say to that?'

But this the Rabbit returned. 'And what would you have expected him to say?'

'I should not have expected a commitment.' The Foreign Secretary was acidulous.

'And you would have been right,' the Rabbit said coolly. 'What I got was a bellyful of high-minded talk and a dissertation upon our common interests.' He stared at the Foreign Secretary reflectively. 'Do you think you could have done better?' he asked.

The Foreign Secretary was silent again.

But the Prime Minister had intervened; he was speaking to the Rabbit. 'This is a matter of impressions,' he was saying. 'May I ask what were yours?'

'In terms, favourable. I don't think our friends are any more anxious to be forced into a position where a decision is unavoidable than are we, for different reasons, in this room. And personally I do not blame them, for a decision under duress is something which any Power is entitled to duck if it can. But you spoke of impressions, and for what it is worth my own are these: our friends will wriggle as they always wriggle. As we would – as we in fact are doing. They don't want trouble and they will probably do a good many things which to us may look shabby to avoid it. But put against a wall they will shoot back.'

There was a considerable silence whilst the Prime Minister looked carefully round the table. 'Anybody to speak?' he inquired.

Nobody spoke.

The Prime Minister returned to Edward Carr. 'Very well,' he said, and he was a little more formal now. 'It is agreed that troops move on to St Cree's. What there are in the Colony are to go at once. You will have to consult with Faulkner, of course, about the future – about reinforcements and so on.' Faulkner was the Minister of Defence. 'We might have to discuss that aspect further in Cabinet. But meanwhile go ahead.' The Prime Minister smiled unexpectedly. 'Do your duty and be damned,' he said. He looked around the table once more. 'Are we agreed?' he repeated.

He spoke as innocently as though he hadn't decided the whole affair, an hour ago in the car from the airport, with Faulkner and the Rabbit. Amongst his several virtues was that he could have made his fortune on the stage.

Edward Carr made a couple of alterations to the draft telegram which was brought to his flat that evening. He removed two commas which he thought tiresome and altered 'considered at Cabinet level' to 'considered by the Cabinet'. Then he initialled in the margin and locked the telegram in its box. The box he returned to the messenger.

He looked at his watch; he had an hour to spare before dinner, and on an impulse he telephoned for the file. It arrived very quickly – the Private Office was efficient – and he saw at once that the matter was as he had expected: the single sheet which had been brought to him was the final of four drafts. A Principal had done the first, and an Assistant Secretary had re-written it; an Under-Secretary had in effect restored the original, and the Deputy had put a little chrome on the result. The Minister reached for his Imperial Calendar. ... It would be a fairly senior Principal, he decided – say seventeen-fifty a year. The Assistant Secretary likewise – say twenty-four and a half. Under-Secretaries and Deputies were on flat rates and the Minister knew them. He knew, too, that nominally – very nominally – all these admirable officials worked a forty-two hour week and had thirty working days of annual holiday. He began a rapid calculation: a Principal cost eighteen bob an hour, give or take a penny or two, and an Assistant Secretary twenty-four shillings. The Under-Secretary came out at twenty-seven, and the Deputy, mightily exalted, at thirty-four. Edward Carr tapped his teeth with his pencil reflectively. He would allow the Principal an hour for his original draft and the Assistant Secretary half an hour for the re-write. That was probably rather conservative, but he did not wish to exaggerate. He wrote down half an hour for the Under-Secretary, but crossed it out again: the Under-Secretary was a notorious fusspot – he must allow him the full hour. For the Deputy a quarter.

The Minister totted up his figures. They came to three pounds ten exactly, and that took no account of light and heat and rent, of typists and office services. Properly cost-accounted the telegram must have cost a tenner before it had reached him.

And he could have done it himself. And so could any competent clerk on three fivers a week.

Edward Carr began to laugh aloud. He was thinking that he was only a Minister: he would go upwards or, more likely, he would simply go out. It didn't matter: he wasn't a Permanent. The system was a joke and, if you took it too seriously, a tragic one. But there wasn't a thing he could do about it – he hadn't the expectation of official life to make it worth a try. They had the drop on him.

He walked to his club for dinner, still smiling at his telegram, unconscious that on the other side of the world it had felled Sir Francis at a blow.

As indeed it had. By the Colony's time it was five in the evening, and by now the Governor had almost finished his decoding, for the message had been in a cipher of which only himself and the Chief Secretary held the Cipher Books. It wasn't one which was used more than once or twice a year, but Sir Francis, in his time, had done his share of ciphering and deciphering, and he was still good at it; he could still make his mind a blank until the message was completed. It was fatal to read the sense before you had finished. You began to assume, to guess. . . .

From: Secretary of State for the Colonies
To: Governor
17764
IMMEDIATE
Topsec. Addressee decipher personally. The disturbances on St Cree's have been considered by the Cabinet. You are authorized to put all available troops on to the island and to restore order with them. Future policy is under consideration. It will naturally be conditioned by developments. I should be grateful if you would report them as they occur and immediately.

There was a good deal more, but this was enough. The Governor read it carefully, and he began to tremble. The fools, he thought once more, the blundering imperialist blockheads, playing at Great Powers, risking the world, risking Sir Francis Eeles. He shivered again, for his ambitions were in ruins. He was naked now, not thinking about Clementi, not thinking about war, but thinking of Francis Eeles and of the future.

Now he had none. . . .

Damn it, they couldn't finish him like this, not those savages, those stupid men. He read the telegram again and his excellent civil-service brain began to work on it. 'You are authorized to put,' he thought – technically that wasn't a formal instruction; technically there was an option. You could stall; you could deprecate. But the Governor was too experienced to deceive himself. Reply to this telegram otherwise than by action and what you would receive would be a rocket. His mouth twisted in distaste, for he was thinking that his Minister, his stupid, his rather commonplace Minister, had a temper; he could write his own messages, and he was capable of a destructive brevity. Reply to this telegram otherwise than by action and what you would receive might even be offensive. . . .

From: Carr.
To: Sir Francis Eeles
MOST IMMEDIATE
Personal
Secretary of State's number 17764. *For* 'You are authorized to put' *read* 'put'. Acknowledge.

No, he wouldn't risk that.

But nor was he resigned to risking his own future, to throwing himself on to the political scrap-heap at the behest of a man whose intelligence he despised. Inferior brains and inferior men. . . . It simply wasn't fair.

Very slowly an alternative came to him – very slowly because it frightened him. Action was imperative and his instructions were formally ambiguous. But play for time and inevitably the ambiguity would be removed for you. Whereupon you would be done for. But whilst it remained you could still take other action. . . .

What other action?

Sir Francis's breath escaped him in a sudden gasp. He would have to go to St Cree's himself.

His handsome mouth twisted again for, with a cynicism which scared him, he was thinking that whilst it would be fatal to become a hero there was perhaps a future in becoming a martyr. A martyr, he thought . . .

He hadn't the least idea what he would do upon St Cree's if he went there. He told himself that he was master of the emollient word, but he could not tell himself that that would be enough. Fear and a lifetime's ambitions tore at him.

He was astonished to find himself before the fireplace of his drawing-room. The telegram and its workings were in his hand. He put a match to them and watched them burn. Very carefully he stirred the charrings with the poker. When they were dust he left them.

He looked at the clock on the mantel: nearly six now – Masters would be at the club. He went to the telephone and summoned him, then crossed to the piano; he began to play one of the Mazurkas, but the Pole's charm had fled. The Governor shut the lid of the keyboard with an irritable bang. He lit another cigarette, though he knew that he had already smoked too many. He had begun to cough, and his doctor had been severe about that cough. He was a man accustomed to take very good care of himself, but now he lit his cigarette deliberately.

He began to pace his splendid drawing-room, waiting for Henry Masters.

The Chief Secretary arrived without comment upon his summons. It wasn't his custom to open such conversations with his Governor as were necessary, and in any case Sir Francis wasn't hesitant in expressing himself. 'I have decided to go to St Cree's,' he said at once.

Henry Masters's habitual expression of detachment changed very slightly. But it was still impossible to read it. 'Very well,' he said.

'And I am going at once.'

'If you had invited my opinion I should have said that the idea was excellent but a little premature. This affair on the island hasn't settled as quickly as we had hoped; there is still considerable confusion. The telephone is working, and from what we hear, though I wouldn't say that the situation is noticeably worse, I can't say that it's very much better either. The Kamblas still seem to be out of hand; they are doing no work; there's still some burning. I can guess what and who is keeping them from settling again. That is also a point which perhaps you should consider.' Masters spoke quite impersonally.

'I have decided to go nevertheless.'

Henry Masters shrugged. 'Very well,' he said again.

'And I want you to help me.'

'But of course.'

'I should like Carey to come with me. I think he ought to.'

'I have heard,' Masters said reflectively, 'that Carey's instructions to Carr two days ago were to leave the island himself and to bring his white assistants with him. Apparently they haven't been complied with.'

'The better reason to go himself now,' the Governor said grimly.

'I agree. But . . . '

'I should be grateful if you would ask him.'

It was in Masters's mind to inquire why His Excellency could not make the invitation himself. But he did not ask the question, for he believed he knew the answer. 'This evening?' he asked.

'If you would not mind.'

The Chief Secretary rose, but he was back in twenty minutes. 'Carey sends you his compliments,' he said, 'and in effect he asks to be excused.'

'Why? Isn't he well?'

'He was starting a cocktail party,' Masters said shortly. 'I was obliged to interrupt it.' He was thinking that in all his life he had never seen two men quite so frightened as Carey and Sir Francis Eeles. In their different ways, of course, and the difference was important. It was also very simple: Carey wasn't going to St Cree's and Francis Eeles was. Harry Masters looked at his Governor with an expression which, if he had noticed it, would have surprised His Excellency considerably. But he did not notice it; he wasn't very good at noticing things; instead he began to talk again.

'Then what about that Associate?' he asked.

Masters shook his head. 'You could hardly approach him.'

'No . . . No, I suppose it would be difficult.'

'For the Associate, very. He could hardly go without consulting Carey. Which would leave Carey with a choice of two courses: he could either go too, and that, if I may be personal for a moment, I'm sure he won't, or he could forbid the Associate to go either. Whereupon the Associate could, we imagine, overrule him, perhaps with and perhaps without direct reference to Brasted. We should have forced him into a crisis with Carey which we have always guessed he is anxious to avoid and which I take it isn't in our own interests either.'

The Governor considered this. 'You are right,' he said finally. 'But I shall go just the same,' he repeated. 'Tonight if possible. Would you see about a launch, please?'

'Carey said he would be pleased to lend you a helicopter.'

'That was very thoughtful of him,' Sir Francis said dryly; he considered again. 'Then I can leave tomorrow morning. At dawn. I shall want the Aide-de-Camp, of course.'

'I will warn him.'

But Henry Masters did not immediately leave; he lit a cigarette, exhaling thoughtfully. Finally he said: 'For what it is worth, my opinion is that you are accepting some risk – a personal risk.'

Sir Francis shrugged faintly. 'It is possible,' he said.

The Chief Secretary stared thoughtfully at the cannas in their magnificent vases. 'I suppose you wouldn't care for me to come with you?'

For a moment somebody peeped from the eyes of Sir Francis Eeles who wasn't entirely an over-ambitious civilian Governor. 'It's bloody good of you,' he said startlingly. He rose, walking to the window, facing but not seeing the baking parterres of Government House. 'Thursday evening,' he said almost to himself. 'Sixty hours, more or less, since Tuesday morning. Sixty hours since the trouble. It feels like a lifetime.'

'You're sure you wouldn't like me to come with you?' Masters repeated.

But Sir Francis had become Governor again. 'I thank you,' he said formally, 'but I must decline. We cannot both be away.'

'Very good,' Masters said once more. He was staring at the cannas again. 'Your Excellency,' he added.

The Aide, next morning, climbed from the helicopter first, helping Sir Francis Eeles. The Governor looked about him in surprise. He didn't quite know what he had expected – not a Police Guard of Honour, perhaps: the police would be pretty busy, he reflected. But at least he had expected the Magistrate and David Carr. A signal would have been sent. ... He didn't quite know what he had expected, but he hadn't expected nobody. There wasn't an official soul in sight, not a soul at all except two men who were walking towards him steadily. He saw that they were strangers. They walked with an air of purpose, quickly but without flurry. They were carefully in step. They came to Sir Francis Eeles, and one man hit the Aide below the ear with what seemed to be a truncheon. He fell without a sound. The other put a pistol in His Excellency's stomach.

Chapter Ten

The reason David Carr had failed to meet the Governor was very simple. He had heard the shot on the veranda and had reached for his pistol as he woke. But the men who were already in his room had given him no chance. They had tommy guns, and David could see that they were expert. One man covered David, but the other did not; he covered the door. They were in uniforms from which the insignia had been cut, but it was evident that they were professionals. In the half-light of dawn their faces were in shadow, but David could see that they were Laramondans. They stood for several minutes, not speaking, until Telemann came in. He made his little bow. 'Good morning,' he said.

David stared at him in hate. 'That shot,' he said savagely. 'My guard . . . ?'

Telemann shrugged. 'I'm afraid so,' he admitted.

'God damn your soul.'

'At any other time the two hypotheses would be extremely tempting. You must excuse me this morning, though. For one thing I am rather busy, and for another I have come to apologize.' Telemann was very sure of himself.

'I don't want your damned apologies.'

'But you misunderstand me. I regret your guard, but I do not apologize for him. Nor that it has been necessary to deprive you of your own liberty – that I am sure you will understand. I came to apologize that I am obliged to take your house. That is a breach of manners, an intrusion, and I am very sorry that it is necessary. You will realize that recent events have made accommodation on St Cree's a little tight. So I am afraid that we shall require your house, or rather part of it. You will be left in your own room, naturally, until the situation declares itself – until we can afford to indulge what is still between us personally. But the rest I need.'

'If I may ask it – what for?'

'For His Excellency the Governor. He is entitled to be housed appropriately.'

'What do you mean?'

Telemann glanced at the bedroom chair. 'May I sit down?' he asked.

'Yes,' David said shortly.

'Thank you. I think I had better explain. This time I can do so with a clear conscience on the score of personal bravado, since the future is now – er, inevitable. Not to put a point on it, I believe we have the situation in hand. But for one point to which, if I may, I will return a little later. But for the moment the position is that His Excellency is about to arrive on St Cree's and that I shall seize him when he does.'

'Forcing the pace a bit, aren't you?' David suggested. But he did not smile.

'I am. Because I must. What has happened is that we learnt last night that Sir Francis had suddenly decided to pay us a visit.'

'Your Intelligence must be pretty good.'

'So you hinted once before. And, as I remarked on that occasion, it has to be. Be that as it may, the Governor was coming. And that was evidently a crisis; that obliged me to take action, and at once.'

'And how will it help you to seize Sir Francis?'

'In a sense it will not – not along the lines of our previous intentions, that is. But in the light of the new situation it would simply be fatal if I did not. What we now need is a hostage.'

'Why?' David asked.

'But surely that is obvious. His Excellency may be arriving because he has already decided that troops should move in. Alternatively he may be coming to see the situation for himself, in which case can you imagine that when he sees it he will not order troops to follow?'

'It is possible . . . ' David began.

'It is certain,' Telemann said firmly. 'Troops,' he went on reflectively. 'They would of course destroy our plans.'

David understood him.

'I can see that you follow me, but for the record I had better be explicit. Clementi intends to have this island; his plans were to acquire it by means of which I was a modest part. Those plans will be useless or at least postponed indefinitely the moment order is firmly restored. So that there had to be another plan, and quickly.'

'And what have you done?' David was thinking that Telemann was extraordinarily confident. Since he seemed willing to answer any questions, he, David, might as well ask them. He had nothing to lose, he thought grimly, by knowing the facts.

'We took the police armoury an hour ago, and now we have taken you. I hope to hear in a minute or two that the Magistrate and your assistants have been dealt with similarly. We shall take Sir Francis when he lands.'

'And the Comingi?'

'There, if I may say so, you made things easy for us. Stout-hearted ruffians at liberty would have been something of a problem – more, perhaps, than we could have coped with. But you will remember that you yourself advised them to stay in the Power Plant till the Kamblas finally quietened. Behind the fence, of course. Which has been very convenient for us, since a couple of men can deal with that. I dare say a few Comingi were outside the wire, when my men set their guns up and, knowing your friends, I wouldn't be surprised if one or two of them chanced it at night. But by and large the Comingi are neutralized. We have given them food and water, of course.'

David thought this over. 'You spoke in the plural,' he said at length. 'You spoke of men.'

'I had a radio,' Telemann explained, 'as I believe you discovered. I still have it. I sent a message to my master, and he dropped me a dozen men.' Telemann waved at the tommy gunners. 'Those are naturally two of them.'

'Why not drop a battalion and make a job of it?'

'Because,' Telemann said simply, 'Clementi hasn't got one.' But he sat squarely on his chair, solid, formidably master of the situation. Presently he said slowly: 'There can be no harm now in telling you our own difficulties. If Clementi had possessed a parachute battalion it would have dropped this morning. That he would have been ready to do, for he was always prepared to occupy this island if the sort of plan which I represented myself should fail. I was the first string, if I may put it that way; I was worth a try. But there is an obvious difference between seizing an open island and fighting for it against troops already in position. A political difference, not a military, for military the affair would have been a walkover. The difference was one between argument and immediate reaction. I do not wish to sound insulting, but Clementi has a poor opinion of your Government, or of most of it; he considered that if he simply occupied St Cree's you wouldn't risk an unlimited war by trying to eject him forthwith. Instead he could oblige you to argue. His people can be loquacious, as I'm afraid I sometimes am myself. You could put it down to the scarcity of intelligent people to talk to – it would be charitable if you would do that.' Telemann smiled a little wryly. 'But though talking is sometimes a failing in all of us, in these circumstances it would have been an asset: Clementi calculated that you would argue before you fought, and we can afford to be patient. History is with us. Whereas if your own troops were already on this island we didn't think quite so badly of you as to believe that you would stomach our cutting them to ribbons. And that is still the position. That is why it is imperative that Clementi should have soldiers on this island before your own. That is why it is unfortunate that he does not have the parachute battalion which you suggested. Even with the arms and training we have given them Laramondans are still indifferent soldiers: the dozen men I have here are something of a *corps d'élite*; they are Clementi's personal guard – Janissaries. But Laramondans are capable of taking this island from a handful of disarmed police, and though they can't jump they can travel by air. And they intend to. The point is simply that we need thirty-six hours to mount the operation – thirty-six hours to what we believe will be finality. Which returns us to His Excellency; which returns us to the point which I mentioned before. . . . My apologies for the speech.'

David shook his head.

'You do not follow me? Then if I may say so, I am surprised. I spoke of His Excellency as a hostage. But there is something more I want of him than that.'

'What?' David asked.

'Time,' Telemann said simply. He looked from the window at the lightening day. 'Time,' he repeated, 'time is of the essence. Thirty-six hours until Saturday evening. I cannot risk it that you beat me to the draw. Thirty-six hours I must have, and Sir Francis can give them.'

'Why the devil should he?'

'Give was of course a very careless word. Yield would be better.'

David looked carefully at Telemann; he did not like what he saw. 'You think you can persuade the Governor to help you?' he inquired.

'Not persuade,' Telemann said. 'Compel.' He looked

from the window again and rose. 'You must excuse me now,' he said. 'I have to meet His Excellency.'

David wasn't greatly surprised when a Laramondan soldier brought him an early but an excellent luncheon and a bottle of beer. That, he reflected, was Telemann all over. He suspected that the meal had been cooked by his own servant: the beer had certainly been iced. He ate the meal thinking about Telemann, careful to think of nothing else. He had heard the noise of the Governor being installed in his sitting-room, a moment of protest, then silence for several hours. After he had eaten he lay upon his bed.

He thought that he had been asleep for perhaps an hour when the Laramondan woke him. He was speaking a sort of Spanish. 'Señor Telemann's compliments,' he said, 'and the Señor would be grateful if you would receive him.'

'Ask him in.'

Telemann came in, his black hat in his hand. 'It is kind of you to see me,' he said.

'What do you want?' David asked wearily; he wasn't in the mood for further talk with Telemann, but he was conscious of the formalities; he wouldn't be found wanting in them and corrected himself immediately. 'What can I do for you?' he inquired.

But Telemann did not answer at once. 'I hope you are as comfortable as permits.'

'I have had an excellent lunch. For which I must thank you.'

'Good. For I feel that my first apologies were perhaps a little inadequate. It is really not my habit to burst into the houses of my equals and use them as hotels.'

'Don't mention it,' David said acidly.

'You are extremely generous; you embolden me. May I trespass on you once more?'

'You hold the whip.'

Telemann looked a little hurt. 'But, my friend,' he said, 'if I may so address you, that is not how I wish you to see it. It has been necessary to confine you – the reasons I need not repeat. But I assure you that there is the clearest distinction between my professional responsibilities and the personal account between us. When the former are completed, when we have leisure, the latter will be attended to. I assure you of that; I assure you most earnestly. I have already promised.' Telemann's expressions changed slightly. 'If no necessity already existed,' he said quietly, 'I could say that you had made it now. I am not accustomed that my word be doubted.'

David Carr looked at Telemann directly. His face was grim, but it was utterly honest. 'It's not your word I doubt,' David said finally.

Telemann's expression broke in an unconcealed relief. 'Good,' he said again. 'Thank you. Then I can ask again for your help.'

'You almost certainly won't get it. . . . What do you want me to do?'

'I want you to see fair play.'

David, now, did not understand him. 'Fair play?' he repeated.

'But naturally. I am about to obtain something from Sir Francis Eeles which I do not doubt he will resist. I am about to compel him, and the essential of the affair is that I should inflict on him nothing but what is necessary. I am not, I think, a coward, and I am therefore not a sadist.' Telemann's mouth shut sharply. 'I am not a professional in this business. I despise them.'

'I see,' David said thoughtfully.

'I am glad. So that I am asking you to witness that nothing is done to your Governor which you would regard as excessive, no means employed which you would think went further than the end which I am obliged to set myself.'

David considered for some time. 'I don't like it,' he said at length. It was an understatement.

'I had hoped to convince you that nor do I.'

David thought again. 'Why don't you ask him first?' he suggested. 'Before you start any tricks.'

But Telemann looked astonished. 'Ask him?' he echoed. '*Ask* him?' He shook his head, evidently puzzled. 'But I have no occasion to insult him.'

David rose, very reluctant indeed; he was thinking that he would probably be sick again. But he would go – he *ought* to go. It could do no harm to Eeles, and it might conceivably do good, spare him something. . . .

They went together into the living-room. The Governor was already strapped on the dining-table. He was in shirt sleeves, and his feet were bare. Two soldiers stood at his head. The Governor did not speak, but his eyes moved miserably. An electric iron stood on an asbestos mat on the table. It was plugged into a socket on the wall.

Telemann began to talk again. 'The objects of inflicting pain can be two: the first could be cruelty and the second is to obtain something which otherwise you would not. That my motives are not the former I do not, to you, think it necessary to emphasize. And as to the latter, you are here to referee.'

'Don't chatter,' David said. 'Get on with it. If you must.'

But Telemann paid no attention. 'I was explaining,' he went on levelly, 'that I am not a professional in this business. I have never had to be, and for that I am thankful. It is not a matter for a gentleman. Nevertheless I have heard something of the theory. Brute pain is a little crude nowadays. It is usually necessary in some degree or other, but it can be minimized. Your object, after all, is to break the will, and there are other means to that. There is dissociation of personality, for instance.'

'Don't talk rot. Get on with it.'

Telemann, surprisingly, did not seem to be offended. 'With your permission,' he said politely, 'I am far from talking rot. I am considering how this incident, which I deplore as you do, can be limited. Permit me to point out that I could have taken one of your cars and gone for a drive; I could have left your Governor to one of these animals here.' Telemann jerked his head at the two Laramondans. 'But I did not,' he added. 'I did not think it proper to.'

David was silent. Privately he was thinking that Telemann had a point. But he did not say so.

Telemann was stroking his chin. 'Music,' he said reflectively. 'I have read that it is often very effective. Play what a man associates with pleasure; play it for some time; then inflict a little pain. Sometimes it need be surprisingly little. It is perhaps worth trying.' He turned to David, evidently relieved. 'Music,' he said again. 'What do you think he likes?'

'I haven't an idea.'

'It would be fatal to be wrong. Play him Count Basie when he is fond of Bach. . . . Do you think he likes Bach, by the way?'

'I don't know.'

Telemann walked to the head of the table, inspecting Sir Francis Eeles; he returned to David. He had excellent manners and, lest the Governor hear him, he spoke in a careful undertone. 'Not Bach,' he said. 'I'm quite sure of that. It's an intellectual's face, of course, but quite undisciplined. And not an Augustan either – not Beethoven, or even Mozart. I should say he was an intellectual romantic.' Telemann snapped his fingers suddenly. 'I have it,' he said. 'Chopin.'

'He does play the piano,' David said involuntarily.

'That is almost corroboration, and accordingly most welcome. Then it is certainly worth the experiment.' Telemann crossed to David's gramophone. 'May I?' he asked.

'I suppose so.'

Telemann brought the side table and the gramophone, putting them beside the Governor. He found a polonaise and put it on. He and David sat together on the sofa. The Laramondans did not move.

David and Telemann sat for some time, Telemann rising to repeat the record as it ran out. The Governor's quick breathing came to them across the room, but still he did not speak. Presently Telemann looked at his watch. 'Purely for myself,' he said decidedly, 'half an hour of that would finish me in any case.' He rose and walked to the table, turning to David. 'Come here, please.'

He took the iron, feeling the heat, like a woman, close to his cheek. David remembered suddenly how superlatively his trousers had been creased when Telemann had returned them. Telemann was handy with an iron. He looked at this one for a moment. Then he drew it once, quite lightly, across the Governor's naked feet.

Sir Francis Eeles screamed sharply.

'But that can hardly have hurt him.' Telemann sounded incredulous; he looked at the Governor curiously. His Excellency's mouth had opened in a sort of blubbering moan. 'Good heavens,' Telemann said. He was astonished beyond suspicion of affectation. 'Good heavens,' he said again, 'it can't be simply the music; it can't possibly work as well as that.' But he put down the iron and walked to Sir Francis's head. 'There is something I want you to do for me.'

The Governor groaned faintly, and Telemann made a signal to one of the soldiers. The Laramondan brought the telephone on its extension. 'I want you to send a message for me. Will you?'

His Excellency did not answer.

Telemann looked at him again; he appeared to come to a decision; he lifted the receiver and gave a number. Presently he said: 'I have a message from His Excellency. For Mr Masters.'

'Speaking,' said the telephone.

'I will put him on.' Telemann put his hand over the receiver, bending to the Governor. 'I want you to say that things on the island have taken a turn for the better; that everything here is under control.' He smiled faintly. 'Say that,' he added, and your difficulties are over. Otherwise . . .'

He nodded at the iron.

A soldier unstrapped one of the Governor's arms, and he took the telephone. Very softly Telemann said: 'Speak naturally, mind. No tricks. . . .'

'Hullo? Is that Masters?'

'Speaking.'

'Eeles here.'

'I'm very glad indeed to hear from you.'

'Things aren't too bad, I find. There's an improvement.'

'Well done.' Masters's voice was generous.

'I can handle it, I think. I'll keep you posted.'

'What shall I tell the Officer?' Masters asked.

'Nothing for the moment. I'll ring again. Good-bye.'

Telemann took back the telephone. 'You did that very nicely,' he said coolly.

*

In the Secretariat building Henry Masters put down the receiver and began to think. He had plenty to think about. The Governor's voice on the telephone, his manner, had struck him as a little odd. Come to think of it, he hadn't much liked the look of him the night before. There had been something about him – strain, evidently, and almost a sort of despair. And, Masters told himself, innocent of cynicism, and it wasn't at all like Francis Eeles to miss an opportunity with the Office. If things were indeed better on St Cree's it wasn't at all Sir Francis's form to keep the information to himself. They might be better *because* the Governor had paid his visit, or it might simply be a coincidence in time: in either case it seemed to Henry Masters very out of character that His Excellency should be hesitating in reporting the improvement. He wasn't a man reticent about his achievements, nor even slow to realize what could reasonably be credited as one.

On an impulse Masters took the telephone again. The Governor would be staying at the Magistrate's bungalow – probably he had taken it over. Henry Masters asked for the number.

He waited some minutes before the operator told him that it was unobtainable.

He lit a cigarette, conscious of an increasing anxiety. Presently he telephoned again, this time to Carey. 'His Excellency rang me this morning,' he said, 'and I have to give him an answer. I've been trying to get him at the Magistrate's, but the number seems to be out of order.' He was being very cagey.

But Carey made it easy. 'That's odd,' he said at once. 'Carr usually telephones about this time, but this morning he didn't. So we tried to get him ourselves, but again we couldn't. Nor the office on the island for that matter. But they tell me the line itself is all right. I can't understand why nobody is answering. Perhaps . . .'

But Henry Masters cut him short; he had learnt what he wished to learn from Carey; he did not desire his reflections. 'Thank you very much,' he said politely.

He finished his cigarette deliberately, for he was in something of a quandary. St Cree's was British territory, part of the Colony, or was claimed to be so. That, he reflected harshly, was what the whole position rested on. So that the Governor was still upon his own ground, still within the jurisdiction. But you couldn't reach him. . . .

Henry Masters wasn't at all a typical civil servant, but he was an experienced one; he took a sheet of paper and began to write a telegram:

From: Chief Secretary
To: Under-Secretary of State
00502
PRIORITY

Personal to Sir John Cadnam. His Excellency left early this morning on a visit to St Cree's. He telephoned at about two, but I think you should know that we have been unable to make contact with the island since.

Henry Masters looked at his watch. . . . Three o'clock by local time: in London the office would be open.

The answer arrived a great deal sooner than he had expected:

From: Under-Secretary of State
To: Chief Secretary
17765
IMMEDIATE

Personal to Henry Masters. Your 00502. Not understood. Are we to understand that the matter referred to in Secretary of State's 17764 has concluded?

Masters sent for his Confidential Clerk. 'Bring me 17764 from the Office, please,' he said. He wrote the number on a slip of paper.

The clerk was back in ten minutes. 'We do not seem to have it, sir. There appears to be a gap. We have received 17763 and 17765 you have before you. But we cannot discover 17764.'

'You're quite sure?' Masters answered.

'Quite, sir.'

'Then thank you.'

Henry Masters dismissed the Confidential Clerk and began another telegram:

From: Chief Secretary
To: Under-Secretary of State
00503

IMMEDIATE
Personal to Sir John Cadnam. Your 17765. I have your reference to 17764 but not your 17764.

The Chief Secretary smiled a little sadly. This, he realized was lucid and succinct: it would excite the pitying contempt of some up-and-coming Private Secretary in the Office. Unconsciously his tongue crept out between his teeth. As well be hanged for a sheep as for a lamb .. . . He added two words to the telegram: 'Repeat urgentest.'

He knew that this was terrible: it was newspaper language —beyond the polite Pale of Whitehall. It didn't matter that it saved a word, it wasn't of consequence that it perfectly conveyed a meaning. And not even 'Please'. . . .

Henry Masters gave the telegram to his clerk.

He lit another cigarette, awaiting the reply. He guessed that it would arrive very quickly, and it was hardly worth starting on other work even if he had felt inclined to. He had supposed that the answer would arrive very quickly, but its format surprised him:

From Edward Carr
To: Henry Masters
17766
SECRET
MOST IMMEDIATE

For Harry Masters. Our 17764 was Top Secret, but the witch-hunt can wait. A paraphrase follows by Savingram, but that isn't important. The instructions were to put troops on to St Cree's and to restore order by force. Eeles's presence on St Cree's does not change them. I should be personally grateful if you would put these instructions in train with topmost priority. Keep me in touch by Most Immediate telegram addressed personally. You may regard yourself as having full powers of Governor and Commander-in-Chief until Eeles returns to mainland and has himself seen and himself repeat himself acknowledged this message. Good hunting, Harry!

Henry Masters read this telegram twice. His wrinkled face broke slowly into relaxation. This was something he understood, this was action. . . .

He picked up the telephone again and sent for the Officer Commanding.

Chapter Eleven

David Carr woke on Saturday morning from a muddled dream. In the huge kitchen of the farmhouse his mother had been ironing his trousers, the iron had got hotter, red hot, though his mother would never have allowed such a thing, and then, senselessly, it was a tank which he had seen in the war, a tank after a brew-up. It had still been too hot to touch. One of the crew, or what was left of him, was still half in the hatch and half out. David had looked at him, and his face had been Sir Francis Eeles's.

He woke with a start, sick at heart and sick of violence. He was resentful and felt he was entitled to be. He was a mild enough fellow, he told himself; he had been bookish once, and even now he was a little quiet. There was a matter to be settled with Telemann, no doubt, but that, though quite unaltered, still imperative, was wholly private. Apart from that he wasn't something from the *Gesta Francorum*, or Don Quixote, or even, in the contemporary idiom, some Private Eye in a Strip. A war had taken him from a life which he hadn't questioned and, since there wasn't any point in being a soldier unless you were a good one, he had done his duty as he had seen it. They had given him a Military Cross, he remembered; they had Belted him. And turned his world inside out in the process. He had discovered a taste for action, a taste through which peeped, mostly at inconvenient intervals, a nostalgia for the other way of life. But he knew that he was fortunate to have discovered himself in time, and as for the occasional regrets, well, falling in love was the conventional remedy for them. Conventional and, in his experience, astonishingly effective. A taste for action, then – action and oil. That was perfectly respectable. Damn it, one could reasonably ask for that without murder and arson and torture, international thuggery. . . .

Damn it, one wasn't that sort of man at all.

David Carr was angry and disgusted.

He looked at the Laramondan soldier who brought him his breakfast. He had his automatic in his right hand and the tray in his left. David, a little incredulous, found that he was thinking that it wouldn't be the least use going for the pistol – the man was trained, a professional: it would be suicide. Whereas he was evidently also a peasant. In his left hand was a tray, valuable crockery, food. . . .

David, dressed now, rose to take the breakfast. Almost unconsciously he kicked suddenly at the tray, and the Laramondan grabbed at it with his right hand. David hit him in the same movement, not bothering with the pistol, somehow catching the tray. He did not want a noise. He took the pistol, quite casually, with his other hand as the man slid slowly down him to the floor. David kicked him once, to make sure. Once, properly, would be enough.

He put down the tray and tiptoed to the door. As he had expected, there was a sentry in the veranda – no, there were two of them, one almost opposite him, the other at the far end. The nearer sentry had another pistol and the farther a sten. David, consciously now, began to think, for it was a nice decision. . . . Take the near man first and the other would still have his tommy gun; he probably wasn't a remarkable shot, but he could spray you. . . . Whereas if you took the sten man first the other was hideously close, he could hardly miss before you turned. . . .

David remembered his own guard dead now. Very deliberately he shot the sten-gunner in the back of the neck, swinging in the same movement on the man with a pistol, firing as he moved his arm, not sighting. He thought that a bullet had come past him, but he couldn't be certain; he was certain, though, that the man with the pistol had fallen. The pistol was at his feet.

David didn't bother with it. He took the sten from the other sentry and he began to run. Once across the compound, he was safe. He knew where he was going, and what he would do when he arrived. And probably so would they. They would race to the bottom of the hills in jeeps; they would block the track to the Valley. David didn't care. They wouldn't catch him on the flat, nor find him on the track in the hills. There were a hundred gullies – gullies, he remembered with amusement, which had been fatal to Carey's ambitions for a proper airstrip. The rain from the hills had eroded them, and to the hills they led. David knew them: Telemann couldn't possibly block them all. And as for the track . . . David found that he was laughing. They could do what they liked about the track: he had walked in the hills, he wasn't too bad on rocks, he could get to the Valley all right. . . .

If he could get across this damned compound.

He hesitated at the wire fence, seeing that it was impossible without cutters, running along it to the gate. There was a good deal of shouting now, and the man at the gate raised his weapon. David, still running, gave him a burst from the sten. He didn't see what happened, but he knew that he was through the gate. A spatter of automatic fire fell uncomfortably close, and David sprinted for the nearest gully.

He began to run steadily, threading his way unhesitatingly through the maze. He was conscious of a stitch and he was delighted; he had a good deal of running to do, and an early stitch was an excellent omen. He would get his second wind the sooner.

And he would get to the Valley. To Jala and to Mr Martin.

But the helicopter beat him. Jala saw it almost at once, running towards it as it landed, expecting David. She was surprised when a stranger climbed from it. He had a hard black hat and very good manners. She didn't think that he was English, but she saw that he was a gentleman. He bowed a little formally. 'May I speak to your father?' he inquired.

'My father is out.'

Mr Martin had gone to one of the old stone forts, the one he kept clear of the wild black bees.

If Telemann was pleased he did not show it. 'It doesn't really matter,' he said, 'for my message is for you. It is from your husband. He would like you to join him at once and has asked me to take you.'

'I'll get my things,' Jala said. She turned towards the little house, noticing that Mr Martin was running down the screes which had tumbled between fort and Valley. He wasn't a man who ran very often; he was waving; he seemed excited.

Telemann saw him too. 'It's very urgent,' he said.

Jala turned again. Unhesitatingly she climbed into the helicopter. Telemann, rather gracefully, helped her.

The machine rose smoothly into the air as Mr Martin reached the beginnings of the Valley. He was shaking his fist; he appeared to be shouting. Jala paid no attention. She was enchanted. The Valley below them diminished, the lush meadows into garden plots, the comfortable cattle into toys. The helicopter moved forward now as it cleared the rim of the hills. In the updraught as they moved over it the machine rose suddenly. Jala gasped and laughed.

She looked about her at the cabin for the first time. There were four of them, she saw – herself, the man who had come for her, the pilot and another. It was a moment or two before she noticed that the fourth man held a knife in the pilot's ribs.

*

Lord Brasted was sitting in the Minister's room, and he was notably less exuberant than was his habit. 'Do you know what really happened?' he asked.

'The telegram left here,' Edward Carr said. 'That has been established.'

'Do you think one of Clementi's agents could have interfered with it the other end?'

'It's possible, I suppose – it can't be excluded. But I'm inclined to doubt it.'

Lord Brasted puffed reflectively. 'You told me it was Top Secret,' he said.

'It was.'

'And that only Eeles and Masters held the Code Books?'

'Yes.'

'So that if Masters had received it his subsequent messages are senseless?'

'I agree.'

'And if Eeles had received it we have still to explain why he ignored it. Moreover it is still to be explained why he should choose this moment to visit St Cree's. With appropriate respect to Sir Francis, and that isn't very much, that is hardly in part.'

'I do not presume to read the mind of Francis Eeles,' Edward Carr said dryly.

'Nor do I.'

The Secretary of State shrugged, and Brasted pulled for some time at his cheroot. 'But it seems to have worked out all right,' he said through the barrage.

'We can hope so, perhaps. They have told us that troops should be moving by about nine this morning. By sea, I'm afraid. Eight or nine hours for the crossing. . . .'

'And meanwhile Clementi . . . ?'

'We don't know what Clementi intends,' the Minister said unhappily. 'That's the rub. He could still get there first.'

'In which case?' Lord Brasted asked. For Brasted he was extraordinarily solemn.

'In which case there is only one course which Her Majesty's Government could adopt – any of Her Majesty's possible Governments. Now, I mean – now that our own troops are moving.'

'I hope I die quickly.'

'So do I. Living in London we probably shall.'

'That is something, I suppose.' Lord Brasted reflected again. 'There's nothing from the Island, I imagine?'

'Nothing concrete. Nobody will answer the telephone yet, but Masters put a helicopter over yesterday evening. It couldn't see anything unusual, and it wasn't shot at. Masters told it not to risk a landing. He was right, I think.'

'Perfectly right.'

Lord Brasted rose, his bulk blocking the window. 'You know, Edward,' he said out of it, 'my first reaction to this affair was to order an aircraft. Indeed I confess I did so. But on reflection' – Lord Brasted chuckled sardonically – 'on mature reflection I decided that a personal visit should be postponed. One Eeles is enough. But I shall go just as soon as you tell me the business is settled. Let me see now. . . . ' Lord Brasted began to scribble figures on an envelope. 'You said that troops would be moving by nine this morning. I take it that meant nine by Colony time?'

Edward Carr nodded.

'Then since it's lunch-time here they should just about have started. Give them your eight or nine hours for the crossing, and two or three more to restore order. . . . Say this evening by their time and about midnight by ours. . . . You'll let me know, I hope.'

'Of course I will.'

'I shall keep awake for the news.'

'I shan't find that difficult myself,' Edward Carr said grimly.

*

Mr Martin reached his house blowing formidably. He went into the veranda and rang his handbell, and at once, from the other houses, men began to stream towards him. There was a surprising number of them, for the Valley had been reinforced. As Telemann had supposed not every Comingo had been confined, and a few, at night, had indeed chanced a shooting. Men native to the Valley had returned to their homes; kinsmen from the Colony had been billeted. They stood in tidy file, and the senior told Mr Martin his story. . . . No, it hadn't been Mr Martin's son-in-law. It had been a stranger. . . . Mr Martin swore at him; he asked what sort of man he considered himself; he insulted him; he blared and he grated; he said things which would have been tolerated on no other occasion.

But now the Comingi did not answer him. They were an understanding and a generous people, and they were sorry for the old gentlemen. Not, they were thinking, that they hadn't a pretty good case in reply; they had taken every foreseeable precaution: the track, where it debouched into the Valley, was guarded, there were look-outs on the hills which dominated it. No drunken Kambla, no hated Laramondan would sneak into the Valley, or if he did he would be more than a little lucky to leave it alive. But a helicopter, dropping from nowhere . . . How could they know? It had been over in an instant.

The Comingi were thinking that they had done their best, but they did not answer Mr Martin. But not because they were afraid to.

Mr Martin finally dismissed them. A little ashamed of himself he went back into the house, falling into the armchair in the living-room, staring at the dreadful oleographs over the fireplace. He was obliged to admit that His Majesty looked positively contemptuous. It was impossible to imagine obscenities upon those bearded lips. A quick-tempered man, they said, but a King, always a King. Mr Martin turned to the other picture, the portrait of the Comingo Hero. He was bearded also, but the growth was sharper, more despotic; the hair sprang from his chin with a precise masculinity. By all accounts he too had been hot-blooded; he would have been every bit as angry as himself and, like himself, he would have needed a butt; but he wouldn't have wasted time in abusing men whom in his heart he knew to be blameless. That formidable dagger, for instance, curved, chased, enamelled. Yes, the Hero would have felt the need to recover himself, the need for violence. A single stroke. A killing. To take life – it was horrible, of course, a sin to be atoned in future lives uncounted; but also it was an attribute of divinity, final and splendid. Putting it bluntly one would be oneself again in no time. Mr Martin smiled as his eyes moved again to the print of His Imperial Majesty the Seventh Edward. Well, he had a sword, hadn't he? Better, that, than a dagger. There was something less than regal about a dagger, something almost domestic. But a sword, now – the sweeping draw, the flourish, the final imperial stroke! Ah, how unhesitatingly he would have accomplished it, how magnificently! No wonder he looked less friendly than usual. Mr Martin had fallen short of his standards.

A sword, Mr Martin remembered. . . . He went into his bedroom, fetching the huge Comingo sword; he sat down again, putting it across his knees. His hands lay on it lightly. He began to think, easily now, lucidly. Presently he rang his bell again, speaking briefly to the assembled Comingi. 'Go to the fort,' he said. 'Take whatever is necessary.'

The Comingi nodded in immediate understanding. 'We hear,' the senior said. 'It is done.'

They were gone in a moment, and Mr Martin returned to his chair and to the sword.

It was thus that David found him, and thus that Mr Martin could tell his story almost calmly.

'My God,' David said.

'We shall be grateful for His help.' Mr Martin spoke respectfully; he had read the Old Testament and he had a substantial opinion of the God of David Carr. After his own, after the Hero and His Majesty. . . .

'And your own tale, my son?' Mr Martin asked David.

'How much do you know already?'

'We know that a stranger, some creature of Clementi's, has been troubling the Kamblas, inciting them. We know that they rioted, drinking and burning. We knew that they were still unquiet, and yesterday two men came back to us saying that Laramondans had come to the island. Soldiers. They were keeping our people in the power plant.'

'They came the night before,' David said. 'They took me too; they locked me up. But this morning I escaped.'

Mr Martin nodded gravely. 'That was proper,' he said. 'That was seemly.' He was speaking in Comingo now. He did not seem interested in the details.

'What are we to do?' David asked miserably. 'Jala – she's a hostage. They've a technique with hostages,' he added.

'She was my daughter,' Mr Martin said simply, 'before she was your wife.'

David was silent and Mr Martin began to think aloud. 'I am pleased that you have escaped,' he said, 'delighted that you are with us. But it does not alter my plans. When we heard that the Kamblas were in riot we took precautions; when we knew that Laramondans were on the island we blocked the Valley; and when Jala was kidnapped I gave certain instructions. We shall now bring her back again.'

David looked at Mr Martin with affection. 'But it won't be easy.'

'We're not scared of a handful of Laramondan pigs.'

'But it won't be a handful; it's going to be an army.'

'My son, I do not follow you.'

'I do not blame you, father. . . . Did you know that the Governor was also on the island?'

Mr Martin was surprised and showed it. 'I did not.'

'He arrived yesterday morning – I don't know why. But the Laramondans took him too.'

Mr Martin considered this. 'To get back Jala,' he said at length, 'is a duty. To free the Governor might well show a profit.'

David couldn't help smiling. 'It isn't as simple as that,' he said again.

'Why not?'

'The Governor's arrival affects this business of an army.'

'Again I do not understand you.'

'The Laramondans, this man Telemann rather, explained it to me. They wanted thirty-six hours to prepare their invasion, thirty-six hours from yesterday morning. Say till early this evening. It was essential to them that nobody should get here first – nobody the Governor might send for. They wanted time – thirty-six hours. So they made the Governor give it them.'

'How?' Mr Martin asked.

David told him.

Mr Martin was evidently astonished. 'Telemann burnt his feet with an iron?' he repeated. 'Once?'

'Yes.'

'And His Excellency telephoned to the Colony? As they asked?'

'He did.'

'It was a disgrace,' Mr Martin said. But he did not make explicit what he considered disgraceful. He thought for some time; finally he said, a little severely: 'You have been wasting our time. None of this makes the least difference to my intentions.'

David managed to suppress his smile. 'May I ask them?' he inquired respectfully.

For answer Mr Martin went to the window. Apparently

satisfied he returned to David. 'Come with me,' he said.

They walked into the veranda, and David gasped. There were thirty or forty Comingi in two respectable ranks and they had just about everything. There was an automatic weapon to every second man, a modern rifle to the other. Three men, a little apart, had what seemed to be a mortar, and it was evident that they weren't strangers to it. Grenades hung casually from leather belts like the parcels of an untidy shopper, and over the little army an air of expectancy. It wasn't the less formidable that it was also a little raffish. At the end of the line was an ancient armoured car.

'My God,' David said again.

'May He attend us.'

David walked down the line, thinking that it wouldn't have done for Guard-mounting. His Regimental Sergeant-Major, speechless, would have reached for the Book; his Company Commander, a Baronet of Ulster and a walking cellar of Scotch, stupid, extremely brave – his Company Commander would have had a stroke. But David was thinking, too, that the stroke would have been unnecessary. There was more to soldiering than ceremonial duties. Which was something the more meticulous Regular was inclined to forget. These Comingi weren't to be despised because they didn't look like Guardsmen, far less because they were merry. They were fighting stock and armed; under their air of fiesta David knew that they were furious, men whose personal honour had suffered an affront, men insulted. Laramondan swine.... Confining them like animals, stealing a headman's daughter ...

David came to the armoured car. A Comingo was at the wheel, and another stood in the open turret. David pointed at the gun. 'Does it work?'

'No sir.' The Comingo sounded aggrieved.

The breech of the gun was rusted solid, but David tapped the armour of the car. It hadn't been painted for a decade, but it seemed sound enough. A two-pounder would smash it to matchwood, but against small-arms fire it would probably hold. The tyres weren't too bad, and the engine, enormous, superbly English, was ticking venerably. There was a sort of steel venetian blind to protect the radiator. David had seen nothing like it outside a museum; he couldn't even guess its date.

He turned to Mr Martin. 'Where did you buy it?' he asked.

'I didn't buy it. I'm not a fool. I took it for a bad debt.'

'How on earth did you get it here?'

Mr Martin looked reflective. 'It is surprising,' he said, 'how far a few shillings will go with a policeman.'

'It might come in useful, I suppose. We'd better take it.'

'Of course we'll take it. It came up the track, by night of course, and it will go down again. Of course we're going to take it.'

With Mr Martin David walked back along the line of Comingi. One of them caught his eye. His head was tied in a white cloth; he looked absurdly youthful. Very discreetly, David attracted Mr Martin's attention. 'He's rather young, isn't he?' he suggested in English.

'He's nearly sixteen.'

'Just the same . . .'

'He's old enough to bear arms. . . . Shall I ask him?'

'If you would.'

Mr Martin addressed the Comingo directly. 'Boy,' he inquired, 'are you a virgin?'

The boy looked flabbergasted. 'No, uncle,' he said. 'Why should I be that?'

Mr Martin waved a hand. 'There you are,' he said largely. 'I told you so.' It was clear that the matter had decided itself; the question was closed.

They walked to the veranda of the house, and Mr Martin faced the Comingi. It was evident that he was about to speak, and David nudged him. 'I would like you to tell them the altered circumstances,' he said.

'What altered circumstances?'

'That there may be more than just a handful of Laramondans.'

'What has that to do with it?'

'Well . . .'

'We're not frightened of Laramondans.' Mr Martin looked at his men dispassionately. 'Of course,' he added modestly, 'I couldn't guarantee to stop a division.'

'I think you ought to tell them just the same.'

Mr Martin shrugged; he began to explain the matter to the Comingi. In the rear rank somebody uttered a loud raspberry. It was a very life-like raspberry: it was difficult to say precisely how it had been produced. The Comingi laughed, and Mr Martin looked at David. 'That is your answer, I think.' He glanced at his watch. 'It is well past midday – we are wasting time again. We must be off. I have something to do first, though.'

He disappeared into the house, returning with the ceremonial sword. One of the Comingi put it into the armoured car, and Mr Martin addressed himself to his men. 'By the left,' he said crisply. 'March.'

It wasn't quite right but it worked. The Comingi did a passable left turn and began to move. Nobody sloped arms: the Comingi carried at the Long Trail, for the Princess of Wales's Own Comingi had been Riflemen and proud of it, contemptuous of silly soldiers who treated their rifles as something to drill with. The tradition was alive still.

David and Mr Martin fell in behind the armoured car. David still had the sentry's sten, and Mr Martin a Mannlicher three-fifty-five. It was his personal property, a beautiful weapon and beautifully kept. He carried it in the crook of his arm, like a shot gun. He had the air, David thought, of an Edwardian magnate taking his house party for a day with the pheasants, and something of the same aura hung about his men.

But it was going to be tough on the birds.

*

The Officer Commanding was sitting with Henry Masters, and both were a little haggard. Major Gage had been up all night, and Henry Masters, who normally slept eight hours like a baby, hadn't slept at all.

Major Gage had been making his arrangements. His two companies of British troops might have been on foreign service a little too long, but they were still efficient. His regiment wasn't a fashionable one: it wasn't Light Infantry or Fusilier; it wasn't Royal or even Somebody-or-Other's Own; but for a very long time it had fought its country's battles wherever on the globe it had happened to find them, and that it was still ready to do. It wasn't a Good Regiment, but it was a very fine one.

Gage hadn't been to the Staff College – he hadn't been accepted. He was aware that acceptance was solely on merit – it must be, for they always said so; but he was conscious, too, that if he had been in God's Own.... But he had decided not to think about that, he had determined not to be bitter. He had missed the Staff College, but he was a most competent officer. He hadn't the aircraft to move by air, and as for the helicopters, there were only two now, and to move in dribs and drabs in circumstances quite speculative wasn't an acceptable military risk. Instead, working through the night, he had embarked his two companies on three launches, their arms, their rations, their impedimenta. At negligible notice it had been a considerable feat. As it happened there was a ship available which would have taken the two companies together, but Major Gage had been properly cautious. Now the two companies had sailed. His instinct had been to go at once with his men, but he had suppressed it: it was better to wait until the second reconnaissance by helicopter that morning. After it had returned he could use it himself. If necessary it could drop him in the sea near one of the launches. Major Gage was forty but very fit.

Now he was telling the Chief Secretary what the pilot of the helicopter had reported. 'It's odd,' he was saying. 'There's still almost nothing to see.'

'Very odd.'

'The only thing unusual is that there seems to be a mass of people in the compound of the power plant. But they appear perfectly orderly. A good deal of stuff is still burning – the pilot couldn't say which of it was new. Naturally he obeyed your instructions not to land or even to go too low. And once again he wasn't shot at. . . . For what that is worth.'

Harry Masters gave the Officer Commanding a cigarette. 'I ought to emphasize again,' he said slowly, 'that I haven't the least idea what you're going into. It may be some sort of local disturbance still, or it may be . . . '

Major Gage nodded. 'I know,' he said simply. 'It may be Clementi.'

'I don't understand it at all.'

'Nor do I. It's twenty-four hours since that message from His Excellency, and in twenty-four hours Clementi could have taken St Cree's. Not by paratroops, perhaps – we believe he hasn't enough. But he could have got there by air. The landing strip is a devil – you couldn't land modern troop-carriers – but some old crate or other, several of them. . . . A determined man who didn't object to casualties . . . '

'Twenty-four hours isn't a long time to prepare a formal invasion,' Masters said thoughtfully.

'We've had to do something like it in less.'

'I know. If I may say so I'm more than appreciative. But Clementi . . . '

'The Laramondan army's pretty fair,' Gage said.

'And its staff?'

Major Gage smiled. 'I think I know what you're trying to tell me. You're saying that we've managed to get moving in under a day and that as far as the helicopters can tell us Clementi hasn't. And you're saying that it doesn't follow from that that Clementi still won't.'

Henry Masters nodded. 'Thank you,' he said. He thought for some time. 'What would you regard as Clementi's dead-line? What time would you give it before we could reasonably assume that Clementi didn't *intend* to move?'

Gage smiled again. 'It's a bit hypothetical, isn't it?' he suggested. 'If we get there first . . . '

'We have assumed, because we must, that if we get there first Clementi won't attack us. But we haven't yet got there first. So what time would you give it . . . ?'

Major Gage considered. 'I guess it at thirty-six hours,' he said finally.

'Which we should calculate from yesterday morning?'

'Yes.'

'Say about six this evening?'

'Yes.'

Henry Masters glanced at his watch. 'What time do you expect to land?' he inquired. But he knew the answer.

'About six this evening,' Gage said.

Chapter Twelve

Mr Martin's little army began to move down the hills. It moved extremely slowly, with an orthodoxy which would have delighted an old-fashioned expert on frontier warfare, a Piffer, but which alarmed and worried David. Mr Martin had been reading something. The armoured car went first, but not before any dominant peak had been picketed. Two or three Comingi would laboriously scale it; would signal the rest of the party forward; and two or three more men, leap-frogging the others, would repeat the manoeuvre on the next hill. It was magnificent, entirely by the book, but it was desperately slow.

David began to fret increasingly. He was fond of these Comingi; he drew strength from their unquestioning confidence; but he had no illusions about pitting them against a professional invasion. It would be wrong to think of such a thing, a crime to allow them to commit themselves. Nevertheless, the little expedition wasn't by any means futile, for against a handful of paratroops there were two objectives which it could reasonably set itself: it could perhaps free Jala and, with great good luck, it might capture a wireless set. And with Jala and the radio it could return to the hills again. It could send to the Colony the information which the Governor had not and, in the Valley, it could probably hold out for several days even against a considerable force – for long enough at least for help to arrive from the mainland. Meanwhile, neither Jala nor a radio was a hopeless objective for courageous men, not hopeless against a dozen lightly armed paratroopers. . . .

Who, David reminded himself, would in a matter of hours be swollen into an army of occupation. Heavy machine-guns, he thought, screw-guns, perhaps even a light tank or two. It was astonishing what you could land by air. And caught on the open plain. . . . He knew his Comingi and they wouldn't flinch: the point was simply that he couldn't permit a massacre.

He looked at his watch: it was nearly four o'clock. He knew better than to protest to Mr Martin, but he pointed at the sun and, to his relief, Mr Martin took the hint. He called down the last of his pickets, nodding at David. 'We must accept some risks,' he said blandly. 'We must press on.'

At the bottom of the hills the police post was deserted. The party moved forward across the plain, quicker now, but still rather slowly, for Mr Martin wouldn't move more than a mile without a reconnaissance. David would have chanced it: Mr Martin would not.

They had gone perhaps two miles across the plain when Mr Martin stopped suddenly; he put up his excellent binoculars, finally handing them to David. 'Look,' he said briefly.

Along the road towards them a cloud of dust was moving quickly. 'I can't see properly,' David said, 'but it looks like a jeep.'

Mr Martin did not answer, for he was making his dispositions. He moved most of his men into dead ground a hundred yards behind the armoured car; the rest he divided into two parties, mostly the men with automatic weapons, one to each side of the car, a little distance away and enfilading it. He was evidently aware that an obstacle uncovered by fire wasn't an obstacle. He and David climbed into the armoured car.

The jeep came very close before it stopped. Mr Martin was fondling the Mannlicher. There was a moment of silence whilst the dust settled; then David said slowly: 'There's a Kambla driving, and two more in the back. They don't seem to be armed.'

'I can see four men,' Mr Martin said.

'So can I.'

'The man with the driver seems to be a European.'

'Ye—es.'

'Do you know him, my son?'

'I think so.'

'Then tell me.'

'I think it is His Excellency.'

'Indeed,' Mr Martin said. He sounded interested rather than surprised.

He put down the Mannlicher as Sir Francis and one of the Kamblas walked slowly from the jeep towards them. 'I suppose,' he said thoughtfully, 'that we ourselves should meet them on foot. I do not understand, but I would not wish to be discourteous.'

He and David climbed from the armoured car. The driver took his pistol from its holster, laying it on the seat beside him.

Sir Francis and the Kambla came towards them. Sir Francis was limping noticeably and David, a little ashamed of the thought, caught himself wondering whether the gesture wasn't rather overacted. The Governor stopped opposite Mr Martin. David he ignored. He took off his hat. 'Mr Martin?' he inquired. 'I was coming to see you.'

Mr Martin bowed respectfully. 'Your Excellency,' he said.

'Don't call me that.'

Mr Martin was a direct man. 'Why not?' he asked directly.

'Because it is not in that capacity that I wish to talk with you.' Sir Francis was talking very quickly; his speech held the hint of a stammer. David didn't like the look at him at all.

'Then what can I do for you?' Mr Martin was very polite.

'I come to you not as Governor, I come as an emissary. I

come with a proposal which I feel sure you will agree is just and reasonable. I think it so myself, or I would not put it before you. I assure you of that. I must make that clear at once.'

Mr Martin thought for some time, his face inscrutable. 'I can't prevent your speaking,' he said finally. 'I must listen.' But clearly the necessity didn't please him.

'Thank you. Thank you very much. Then my proposal, if you accept it, will restore your daughter.' For the first time Sir Francis seemed to notice David; he gave him a brief, a reluctant bow. 'And your wife, I hear,' he added.

David was silent; he was more than content to leave the talking to Mr Martin.

Mr Martin, now, wasn't looking at the Governor. 'May I put you a question?' he asked. He was being very careful with his English.

'But of course.'

'It is a little personal perhaps. You will forgive me. . . . Did they burn you again?'

Sir Francis dropped his eyes. 'No,' he said at last.

'But they threatened to?'

'Yes. . . . Yes, they did.'

Mr Martin withdrew his gaze from the coppery sky. 'Say what you have to,' he said.

'Thank you again. It is quite simple, really. Clementi – the Laramondans, you know – are landing on this island in a matter of an hour or so. We guessed that you might be coming. . . . They do not want to fight unless they have to.'

'That I can understand.'

'So I have been asked to make you a proposition. I must insist that it is a fair one, one which I myself . . . '

'Make it short,' Mr Martin said astonishingly.

'I am sorry, I . . . ' Words began to tumble from Francis Eeles, undisciplined, unsyntactical. This wasn't the Governor and it was horrible. 'Go back,' he said. 'Return. To your

Valley. You will be left in peace. Go back and I will bring your daughter to you. Here. I can deliver her, I promise it. Later there can be talk about the island. Proper talk. The diplomatic channel. . . . '

Mr Martin pulled his beard. 'The island is not yours,' he said curtly. 'You hold it for another.'

'I know, but . . . '

Mr Martin, for the first time, frowned. 'And if I refuse?' he asked levelly.

'But you cannot refuse – it is a madness. Soldiers are coming from Laramonda. By air. Proper troops. What chance . . . ?'

Mr Martin looked at the sky again. 'Haven't you thought that there are also soldiers in the Colony?'

'What difference could they make? Even if they were coming. Two companies against an army. Fighting, useless bloodshed. . . . '

'If they aren't coming it's because you haven't sent for them.'

'But I was compelled,' the Governor began miserably.

But Mr Martin interrupted; he said something in Comingo which David didn't catch. It sounded like a quotation.

'I entreat you,' Francis Eeles began again.

Mr Martin held up his hand, considering his next question. His English became formal again. 'Do I understand,' he asked slowly, 'that if I agree to return to the Valley you will deliver my daughter unharmed?' He seemed relieved that the sentence had been successfully delivered.

'Yes. Yes, I said so.'

'And that my people will be left in peace?'

'Yes. Of course. Certainly.'

'Whereas if I decline . . . ?'

The Governor dropped his eyes again. 'Your daughter,' he said to the dusty earth, 'your feelings as a father must oblige you . . . '

'I see,' Mr Martin said reflectively. 'I see.' He thought for a full minute before he spoke again. 'And yourself?' he asked at last. 'If I agree, they will not harm you?'

His Excellency did not raise his head, but he nodded.

'But again if I refuse . . . ?'

The Governor did not speak. David, entirely embarrassed, saw that he was weeping.

Mr Martin pulled his beard again. 'Come with us,' he said suddenly. He was determined to be fair. 'Make a fight for it. Lead us,' he added magnanimously. It was an effort, but he said it.

'But it is hopeless. A handful of peasants . . . '

Mr Martin sighed profoundly. He seemed to shrink as the breath left him, and more than physically. Virtue had gone out of him, some trust, something never questioned. In its place was an illusion acknowledged, and he walked with it, a little bent, to the armoured car. He took from it the ceremonial sword, feeling its power meditatively with his enormous hands. Something from his boyhood, something learnt at a Company school, came back to him. He drew a deliberate breath. 'So perish all traitors,' he said. His voice was deep and formal and utterly impersonal. The sword, suddenly, in his huge hands was alive. It was something almost visible.

Mr Martin, for some moments, stood entirely still. Then slowly he shook his head. 'I cannot,' he said simply. 'I will it but I may not judge.' He was speaking in English still, but thinking in Comingo.

He made a sign, and two of the Comingi held Sir Francis Eeles. 'Take him to the Valley,' Mr Martin told them. 'Put him in the Fort. Guard him.'

He turned to the Governor again, and his voice was resentful; he had been cheated and he hadn't forgiven. 'You will be quite safe with my people,' he said scathingly. 'Do not fear.' He whirled on the attendant Kambla, his rage and broken trust exploding. 'Back to your masters,' he said furiously. 'Give them my answer.' He raised the sword six inches, and the Kambla turned and ran.

David watched the dust of the jeep as it faded across the plain.

Very deliberately Mr Martin returned the sword to the armoured car. David was looking upwards, for he thought he had heard an aircraft. He searched the sky but could see nothing, nothing beyond a sun ominously low. On St Cree's it was day in one moment and night in another. He walked to Mr Martin, pulling at his sleeve; he would have confessed that he was a little apprehensive.

'Well, my boy?'

David pointed at the sun again.

'Quite,' Mr Martin said. 'Quite so.'

'Father, I think we should be reasonable.'

'But of course.'

David began to explain what he considered possible; he did it tactfully, for he thought it wise to. 'I don't think we ought to try too much. These Laramondans are due in under an hour and we don't know how many there will be. But in an hour we could do plenty.'

'We shall have to,' Mr Martin said grimly. 'Those Kamblas will be back by now to whoever sent them, and Jala . . . '

'Exactly. We ought to get her at once. Immediately. And one other thing if we can.'

'What's that?'

'A radio.'

'I see,' Mr Martin said thoughtfully.

'We could go back to the Valley and send a message to the Colony. In the Valley we could hold for several days. Against anything Clementi could send.' David wasn't at all sure that he was right, but he was exercising a simple cunning.

Mr Martin considered, but not for long; he was a man

who made decisions easily. 'You are right,' he said. 'And first things first – Jala, that is. Where will they be keeping her?'

'Probably in my bungalow, since it's about the only building still with a roof on. Telemann is very considerate, you know. In his way.'

'There's nothing much between ourselves and that house of yours,' Mr Martin said.

'Nothing much. It's lucky it's on this side.'

'No house-to-house fighting to get at it?'

'I shouldn't think so.'

'Nothing eats men like house-to-house fighting,' Mr Martin said professionally.

'I know.... We shall have the airstrip on our left, of course. Flanking us. But it's open ground. I shouldn't think they'd trouble to occupy it even if they had the men.'

'Nor should I.' Mr Martin threw away his cigarette, turning to the Comingi. He explained, and very quickly. 'Keep behind the car, and take any cover there is. But we haven't time to look for it.'

The Comingi nodded, and David and Mr Martin climbed into the armoured car.

They were perhaps a thousand yards from the bungalow when the shooting started. It was a shell from a mortar, a hundred and fifty yards short. The driver stopped. Two seconds later another burst a hundred and fifty yards behind them. David shook the driver. 'Go forward,' he said urgently. The driver let in the clutch, and the third shell fell neatly where the car had stood. 'Very pretty,' David said respectfully. 'Very good bracket indeed.'

Mr Martin was looking at the Comingi. They had scattered, taking the sparse cover that offered. But they weren't firing; they were waiting for orders. 'I didn't think they would have mortars,' Mr Martin said coolly. 'But we shall have to get on.'

'No.' David was staring at the sky again, and this time he could see it. 'Look,' he said.

It was a fighter, not made in Laramonda but with Laramondan markings. It was going very fast, sweeping the airstrip in surprisingly tight circuits, very low, banked almost vertically.

'He's good,' David said.

'He can't possibly land.'

'I don't think he's trying to. He's making a recce.'

Two more shells, less than two seconds between them now, bracketed them again neatly. 'Move,' David said.

The driver moved.

'We shall have to get on,' Mr Martin said again.

But David was speaking to the driver. 'Get her hull-down,' he told him. 'They may bounce one on us, but it's a fluke if they do.' He shouted at the Comingi, pointing at the tail of a gully. 'Get in there,' he said. 'Wait.'

'What the devil . . . ?'

It was Mr Martin, very angry, but David interrupted him. He hadn't meant to take charge, he had told himself that above all things he mustn't. But he had. He turned to Mr Martin, his manner a blend of authority and deprecation. 'Father,' he began.

But Mr Martin was laughing hugely; he wiped his eyes with an excellent linen handkerchief. 'All right, my boy,' he said. 'All right. I was expecting it, really. . . . What do we do now?'

'I'm sorry, I . . . '

'Don't waste time, boy. What do we do? What do *I* do?'

The fighter was still ringing the airstrip, and David jerked his head at it. 'He's not there for nothing,' he suggested. 'There'll be somebody behind him.'

'There is.'

'Where?'

Mr Martin tut-tutted. 'I am older than you,' he said, 'but

I have much better eyesight.' He handed David the binoculars. 'There,' he said briefly.

David looked carefully. 'I make it six,' he announced. 'Old Dakotas, I think. Yes. . . . No. . . . '

'Very interesting,' Mr Martin said acidly. The laughter had discharged him; he was himself again.

'They could land, I think, or one or two of them might.'

'What are you going to do?'

'I'm going to turn you out of this car.'

'Never.'

'Join the men. Wait for me.'

Mr Martin fought with himself what was evidently a battle. 'I suppose I agreed,' he admitted reluctantly. 'In a way. . . . '

David turned to the driver. 'Go, too,' he said, 'but return Bring me a dozen grenades. All sorts.'

'Sir.'

The shelling had stopped as Mr Martin and the driver climbed from the armoured car. Telemann, David reflected, would consider the situation well in hand: shooting at a halted enemy would be superfluous. Mr Martin, with great dignity, unnecessarily, walked to the gully. But the driver returned at the double. He had what David had asked for and he put them in the armoured car. 'May I come, sir?' he asked.

'I'm afraid not. But thank you.'

The Comingo retired to the gully with the air of a dog hopeful of exercise and disappointed.

David began to think again, for he wasn't at all sure that this would work. He could get to the well, all right: the chances of hitting a moving target with a mortar weren't at all good, and against small-arms fire he had already decided that the ancient armour would hold. Once arrived, of course, he would have to get out; he would have to take his chance and he was ready to. . . . Yes, he could get to the well with any luck, but he wasn't quite certain that he could fire it.

Carey, he remembered, had once talked largely about wells on fire. Montez had gone in the night and Montez had caught. . . . 'It caught, of course – they nearly always do like that. . . . ' It had been nonsense: Montez had been an exception. Wells mostly caught when the drill was in them, and devils they were. Sometimes you had to blow them out. An admirable Texan charged you thirty thousand for the job when it was beyond you. He sometimes *blew* them out – that was the point and that the doubt. Now you were putting a string of grenades round a Christmas Tree and pulling the pin. You could leave the armoured car for good measure, no doubt, an extra grenade under the tank. That would certainly catch. . . .

David held up his handkerchief, testing the wind. Yes, it was across the airstrip. It might work, it ought to work. . . .

It *must* work.

He was half across the airstrip, driving very fast, before the firing began again. They weren't bothering with the mortar, but the bullets began to thump against the plating. David listened to them almost nostalgically. He had decided not to worry about the armour and he wasn't worried. But the tyres. . . . He was a good deal less than broadside to the fire which came at him, but he knew that he was vulnerable. Shoot him out of air and he was a sitting duck for the mortar.

He found that he was at the well and he backed the armoured car against it. The petrol tank was at the rear. He dropped the grenades from it, jumping himself, taking what cover the car afforded. The automatic fire was persistent and accurate, but he piled his grenades round the base of the Christmas Tree, the last under the car's petrol tank. He pulled the pins from two, turning to the last under the car. For a moment the pin stuck: David's stomach turned over. Then it was suddenly in his hand. He began to run. He was conscious that behind him men were moving across the airstrip, shooting, firing from the hip. David wasn't frightened of them but he was frightened. He ran as he had never run.

He heard the explosion and threw himself flat; he turned in the dust and gasped. Carey, he thought again – Carey had been right in one thing. 'A wall of flame,' he had said, 'a fountain of fire,' and David had been obliged to suppress a smile. But now he was not, for he did not feel like smiling. A spout of burning oil clawed at the sky; bent in the wind like a knight's plume; fell finally across the airstrip. The men on it had disappeared.

Seventy thousand a day, David found himself thinking, seventy thousand barrels. He had thought it an almost certain exaggeration. Now he would believe it.

He rose to his feet but instinctively dropped again. One of the Dakotas was coming in. He could see that the pilot was fighting to pull out. But he was committed. David would have liked not to look. The aircraft rose for a moment, dully, sluggishly. He's going to stall, David thought. The aeroplane dipped suddenly; disappeared in the curtain of burning oil. In an instant it had emerged but it was no longer an aircraft. David, now, turned his head. He heard the crash and another explosion, and when he looked back it was over.

David rose for the second time. He found that he was a little shaky. He looked at the roaring well, and he looked at the airstrip: what wasn't already a pool of flame was blocked by the Dakota's blazing wreckage. Then he looked at the sky again. The fighter was leading away the five Dakotas.

David, at a double not quite steady, made his way back to Mr Martin through the gullies which ringed the airstrip. The Comingi were staring at the well, silent, shaking their heads. They were a provident people, they hated waste, and this was waste unimagined and unimaginable. But Mr Martin was chuckling. A little formally he shook David's hand. 'Well done.'

'I was lucky.'

Mr Martin produced a splendid silver flask. 'Drink,' he said, 'and give us our orders.' He was a little sarcastic, but not very. 'It is a trap, no doubt.'

David drank gratefully. 'What's a trap?' he asked.

For answer Mr Martin stood up, pointing at David's bungalow. 'Look,' he said.

Rather more circumspectly than Mr Martin, David looked from the gully at the bungalow. It was perhaps half a mile distant, and he borrowed the binoculars again. 'It's a white flag, all right.'

'So I can see. The question is what we do.' Mr Martin glanced at the airstrip. 'I think we can take it the Laramondan army isn't coming,' he suggested.

'Not by air, anyway.'

'And of those bastards here already I saw four run out on to the airfield. I didn't see them come back.'

'I'm sure they didn't.'

'And you spoke of a dozen originally. And two you shot. Six from twelve leaves six.' Mr Martin nodded at the bungalow. 'Perfectly open ground. Not a blade of cover. Six men shooting over that could make mincemeat of us. I wish we still had that car – the car you burnt.' Mr Martin wagged his head reprovingly. 'You shouldn't have done that,' he said. 'It cost me a hundred pounds.'

'You said you took it as a bad debt.'

'I did – for a hundred pounds.' A thought occurred to Mr Martin and it appeared to cheer him. 'I shall claim,' he announced. 'I shall claim from Her Majesty's Government.'

'I doubt you'll get a penny.'

'Shameful!'

David smiled. 'But you needn't worry. The Company will pay.'

Mr Martin was evidently relieved. 'Ah,' he said. 'The Company . . . of course.'

But David had been thinking. 'We can get a good deal

nearer under cover,' he said. 'I know where this gully goes. A branch comes out quite near the bungalow. I know because I used it when I – when I came up to you.'

'Then we'll use it too.'

David led the Comingi, but slowly, halting at the intersections, reconnoitring the corners. Presently he stopped. 'This is as near as it goes.' Very cautiously he peered over the parapet. 'Seventy yards to the gate. It doesn't seem to be manned. Then across the compound.'

'We'll rush it,' Mr Martin said.

'No.'

'What do you mean, no?'

'It's the worst thing we could do.'

'Do you expect us to march it in drill order?'

'No again. I think it would be better for one man to go. Myself in fact.'

'Never,' Mr Martin said again. His voice was quite final.

'But Jala . . . '

Mr Martin exploded again. 'Stop talking about my daughter,' he said savagely. 'I know she's in there, I know what could happen – may have happened.' He was panting. 'You come to my house and you marry my daughter. You sleep with her for a single night and you disappear. You mix yourself up in God knows what and when you return she is gone. Is that proper or seemly? Is that a decent son-in-law?'

It was utterly unfair, but David wasn't angry: Mr Martin had given him an idea. 'You are in my debt,' he said quietly.

'I owe no man a penny.'

'You owe me a dowry.'

Mr Martin stopped as though he had been shot. 'Dowry,' he said indignantly. 'Dowry! A fine time to start talking about dowries.' But he was evidently shaken. 'There's hardly been time. . . . '

'I know. But you owe it still. You're a man of principle.'

'I should hope so.'

'Then pay me now. Let me go. I'll take that instead.'

Mr Martin stood extremely still. 'It's blackmail,' he said at length. 'Dirty blackmail.'

'Call it legitimate pressure.'

'Call it what you will. I don't like it.'

'Call it a bargain then.'

But Mr Martin, unexpectedly, wasn't looking at David. 'You're a devil,' he said to the wall of the gully. 'I like you very much.' He turned to David Carr again. 'Very well,' he said in Comingo. 'I'll settle with you later, though. I concede your right but not the bargain. Bring the daughter that goes with it. Bring your wife.'

David climbed from the gully and began to walk towards the bungalow. He had never felt so naked nor so frightened. A little ashamed he discovered that his knees weren't quite reliable. But he forced himself on, not thinking. He reached the gate and went through it, across the compound. He was coming in by the back, to the veranda where the sentries had stood over him. The door into the living-room was shut, and David halted outside it, thinking now, remembering. He had learnt about this once – once, in another life. He stood against the wall, beside the door and away from the hinges. It wasn't a heavy door and it opened at his second kick. Now he could see half the room and there was nobody. . . .

He moved quickly across the open doorway to the opposite side. . . . The other half of the room now, and there was nobody again. But there was still something to make sure of. The door wasn't flat against the wall, and they had warned you about that, they had demonstrated. It had been rather painful. David, very carefully, swung the door right back on its hinges. It came against the wall. Nobody. . . .

He went into the room and the blow caught him brutally on the crown of the head.

When David came to Telemann was bending over him. He had a bucket and a sponge, and he was being very gentle. He was smiling. 'You shouldn't have fallen for that,' he said.

'What happened?' David asked. It was a banality and he was aware of it.

For answer Telemann pointed at the doorway. Above the lintel was a narrow wooden shelf. Alone it wouldn't have supported a man or even a man's weight, but above it two loops of rope had been screwed to the composition wall. Telemann smiled again. 'It's an oldie,' he explained. 'You should have known it. . . . I was obliged to, you know. You might have come in shooting – making trouble. It would have been extremely awkward.'

'What have you done with my wife?'

'Nothing.'

'Where is she?'

'I put her in your bedroom. You will not misunderstand me if I say that it seemed the best place.'

Telemann was extraordinarily gay. He threw the sponge into the bucket and crossed to the bedroom door; he unlocked it. 'Come in, please,' he said. 'Your husband has arrived.' He held the door for Jala politely.

She ran to David and he saw at once that she was unharmed. He held her, not speaking. Telemann, a little studiously, was looking from the window. He was humming softly.

'What now?' David asked.

'Rather a lot perhaps.' Telemann looked at his watch. 'But we have time to proceed decently. Just.' He moved to the table, opening a bag, producing a bottle and glasses. 'Brandy,' he said. 'Good brandy. As good or better than you gave me. I cannot express the pleasure, the relief, with which I offer it.' He poured three glassfuls, giving one to Jala and another to David. He bowed to Jala. 'Your very good health.' He raised his glass.

Jala was watching David; when she saw that he was drinking she followed him.

'You're in very good form,' David said. He had never seen Telemann so carefree, and he was puzzled.

'But of course I am. I have failed. I am free.'

David shook his head. 'I don't understand,' he said.

'But my dear fellow! You have successfully blocked the airstrip, and I congratulate you. It was really quite a *coup*. Which means that Clementi cannot land, or at least not tonight. And it has to be tonight.'

'Why?'

'Because your own soldiery is itself arriving in a quarter of an hour'

'I didn't know that.'

'You couldn't. But our own Intelligence . . . '

'Your excellent Intelligence,' David said. He was surprised to discover that he was himself smiling: Telemann's gaiety was irresistible. But he shook his head again. 'I still don't follow why you're so pleased. I should have thought . . . '

'You would have thought both right and wrong. I am distressed, naturally – professionally a little humiliated – that I have failed. But the failure has compensations. I was sent here – lent here – for a particular purpose. I have failed in it lamentably. I could not return even if I wanted to. You will understand that. I cannot return, but I do not wish to. There is something more important, and that I can now attend to. This is the end of the man called Telemann. That, if you will forgive the word, that is ineluctable. This is the end of Telemann. What I was I am again. And that is important for it is all that is left me.'

'Who are you?' David asked.

For a moment Telemann hesitated; then he went to a chair and picked up his black hat. He did something to it; he straightened the brim and the crown he made quite flat; he put the hat upon his head and at once he was another man.

He took it off again, making a sweeping bow at Jala, ending with the hat above his heart. 'Your servant,' he said.

He began to introduce himself. The splendid rubric rolled from his tongue. There were a great many 'de's' and something about la Torre. The recital took a considerable time. It ended in Fontana.

David snapped his fingers. 'Fontana,' he said. 'But of course.'

Telemann looked surprised. 'We have met before?' he inquired.

'Once or twice.'

'May I ask where?'

David told him, and Telemann's face fell. 'I would have preferred almost anywhere else,' he said sombrely.

'I don't see why.'

'Because I am ashamed.'

'But to be Counsellor of Embassy in London – I should have thought that was something.'

'It was. In the circumstances it was a disgrace. In the circumstances ... my circumstances.'

'I shouldn't have felt that way about it.'

'No doubt. But then you are not a Spaniard.'

'Nor a grandee of Spain,' David said.

Telemann looked surprised again. 'How did you know?' he asked.

'But you've just told me.'

Telemann laughed. 'If you know enough of Spain to recognize my name you should know enough to understand me.'

'I'm afraid I don't. I'm quite at sea.'

'Being a grandee isn't the point: it's being a Spaniard. When we change our politics we ... we change them. No comfortable Anglo-Saxon compromises. We're extremists, nature's out-and-outers. We can't help ourselves; we go the limit.'

'And what was *your* limit?'

'My limit was that Fontana became Telemann.'

'I see,' David said; he rubbed his chin. 'I think I see.' He stared from the window: Mr Martin was invisible, still in the gully. At last David said slowly: 'You're an anachronism. I admire you.'

'*Admire* me?'

'Assuredly.'

'I was right,' Telemann said. 'You are a gentleman. The final test of that estate is to lie gently.' He returned to the table, pouring more brandy. Jala declined, and Telemann did not press her. 'Your health,' he said once more.

'Fontana's very good health.'

Telemann laughed again and David smiled. It was absurdly important that Telemann shouldn't be unhappy. He hadn't much longer to live.

They drank their brandy, at ease, almost cosily. Finally Telemann said: 'But being Fontana isn't quite irrelevant. Telemann is destroyed, but Fontana is re-created. Fontana has certain obligations, and I can pay them. A little brandy was the least of them. Quite the least.'

'Yes,' David said. Instinctively he put his hand to his neck. It hadn't been too bad the last few days: he had had something else to think about; he hadn't woken sweating in the night. But now he put his hand to his neck. 'Yes,' he said again.

Telemann noticed the gesture. 'My apologies. You have them already and they are not enough. You saved my life, and you were garrotted in London.'

'You warned me.'

David was determined to be judicial.

'I knew of the affair and could have stopped it. I did not know its nature or I should. I need not tell you that, I hope.'

'You need not.'

'You are generous. I have a horror of the wire.'

'So have I,' David said. He meant it.

'I owe you a life,' Telemann said. 'I owe you the opportunity.'

'You promised it. I never doubted.'

'I thank you.'

Telemann turned to Jala. 'Madam,' he said, 'we are being discourteous. We have been boring you.'

Jala was sitting silently, not following quite all of this, but following enough. She was thinking that men, even good men, and this stranger was evidently a good one – men were incomprehensible. Men were beyond understanding, but they were men. Something was happening, something between men. It would be stupid to interfere. She gave to Telemann a tiny sitting bow. 'Not at all,' she said politely.

Telemann moved to the table again but stopped short of it; he seemed to be listening. 'Do you hear it?' he asked.

David had not, but now he did. It was firing, and it was coming from the harbour. 'Your soldiers have arrived,' Telemann said.

'But what are they firing at?'

'What is left of my men.' Telemann sighed. 'Like myself,' he explained, 'they cannot return. They can hold up your soldiers for ten minutes, I dare say, and they can die. Ten minutes – it is enough if we are quick.'

'Let us be quick then.'

'But not indecently. There should be Seconds, a Cartel – that is impossible, of course. But there must be order. One thing is certain: you have choice.'

'But no experience of the occasion.'

'Have you ever used a sword? I have brought a pair.'

'Never, I'm afraid.'

'Then if you will permit me to advise you, do not choose one. As a swordsman I am unremarkable, but I am a swordsman.'

'Firearms?' David suggested.

'Perfectly in order, of course.' Telemann returned to the table, opening his bag again, producing a flat case. He brought it, open, to David. 'Beautiful, aren't they? Made in London, naturally. The upper killed my grandfather.'

'Do they fire?'

'I must admit that by now they are not quite reliable. There is the question, too, of protocol – of paces and firing. There should be a Controller. . . . Revolvers, you will agree, any automatic, would merely be barbarous.'

David heard himself saying: 'Of course.'

'Which leaves me inviting your choice still.'

David reflected. Unconsciously he put his hand to his throat again, discovered the gesture and was irritated by it. There was nothing there, nothing but a shuddering recollection. He hadn't even been marked – not on the throat, at least. There was that scar on his cheek, but that was different, that was . . .

'Bayonets,' he said suddenly. He wasn't at all sure that he hadn't said something disgraceful.

But Telemann was scratching his chin. 'I don't see why not,' he said after a moment. 'Steel is perfectly respectable, perfectly in tradition, and though I confess never to have heard of such a thing I can see nothing against it. I *feel* nothing against it. Steel in the hand is a sword. Steel on the end of a stick is still a sword.'

'Rifle Regiments call it so,' David said thoughtfully.

'So they do. . . . That is settled then. As it happens we shall find what we want in the other veranda.' Telemann smiled his gayest smile. 'They belonged to the men you destroyed. The animals. They left their toys behind them.' He began to walk to the veranda.

'Wait,' David said.

Another burst of firing came to them from the harbour. 'We haven't too much time,' Telemann said.

'You asked me whether I could use a sword. Have *you* ever used a rifle and bayonet?'

'Of course.'

David looked at Telemann very carefully. 'You're not telling the truth.'

Telemann smiled again, but he did not protest.

'We'll have to toss,' David said.

'Toss or draw.'

'Draw then.'

Telemann went to the table once more. He tore two slips of paper, and David watched him write 'sword' on one and 'rifle and bayonet' on the other. He folded the strips carefully; he put them into his black hat, and the hat he took to Jala. He bowed. 'Madam,' he said, 'do us the honour to draw.'

Jala looked at David and David nodded. She took one of the pieces of paper and handed it to Telemann. He unfolded and read it. 'Rifle and bayonet,' he announced.

He put the paper into his pocket and went into the front veranda. The weapons he returned with were modern rifles. Their bayonets, too, were very up-to-date. They were hardly more than knives, but they were deadly. 'They're identical,' Telemann said. 'But choose.'

David took the nearer, looking at Jala. She sat quite still, her hands crossed on her splendid bosom. Her eyes were shining. Telemann followed David's glance. 'My congratulations.'

'Thank you.'

'On guard.'

'One thing,' David said.

'What now?'

'You're not obliged to meet me, you know.'

'What do you mean?'

'Your father was Fontana: mine was a farmer.'

Telemann grounded his rifle; he leant against it, laughing uncontrollably; he wept and he gasped, and when he spoke it was with difficulty. 'I know he was,' he said. 'He had four hundred acres.'

'Yes.'

'But he owned it, didn't he?'

'He did.'

'And your father's father?'

'Yes.'

'My friend, that is the point. He owned it.' Telemann began to laugh again. 'I intend no discourtesy, but you are very funny. I spent five years in your country and at the end your social hierarchy was still inexplicable. So I clung to one thing – I clung to my own. A man who had land was a gentleman and a landless man was not.'

'It is a considerable over-simplification,' David said. He said it a little stuffily. People, Jala for instance and now Telemann, had the oddest ideas about land. For himself he had always taken it for granted. It hadn't been a matter of mystique: it was something to live on. Well, he was learning. 'It is an over-simplification,' he repeated.

'I do not doubt it, but it will do for me. It would have done for my father.'

'Your father would have fought a duel? Your *father*?'

'Most certainly he would. The affair would have had to be discreet, of course. But he would have accepted a challenge.' Telemann looked at David a little curiously. 'More important in this context, if he had felt an obligation he would have offered himself.'

David in turn considered Telemann. He couldn't decide whether he loved or hated him. But he was still determined to be fair. 'You spoke of your father,' he said. 'That would be years ago.'

'Thirty,' Telemann agreed. 'But nothing in seven hundred. I spoke of my father but I speak for myself.'

Outside the bungalow there was a sudden shouting. British voices were raised with Comingo.

'You're an anachronism,' David said again. 'You're rather frightening and rather splendid. But I think you were happier dead.'

'I am willing.'

'On guard then.'

'Ready.'

. . . . Short point, long point, short point. Feeling . . . Telemann had indeed been lying; he didn't know a thing. He was fighting by instinct, meeting the points as David might have met a sword, by reflex. The simplest feint . . . David knew he could take him when he wished to. Well, he wasn't going to murder – Telemann should have his chance. He risked an overpoint, and now he did not miss. Telemann fell at once, the bayonet in his throat. He was still smiling.

Jala rose smoothly, striding to Telemann, kneeling beside him. For a moment David did not see what she intended. Then he leapt at her, catching the knife. He was wondering where she had been keeping it. 'No,' he said vehemently. 'You can't do that. No.'

He seemed to have been saying No to Comingi rather a lot lately.

Jala fought him furiously. 'He might have killed you,' she said, choking. Her face was twisted, unrecognizable.

'He's dying,' David said. The bayonet had cut the jugular. It was true.

For another moment David thought she would turn the knife against himself. Then she rose slowly. He saw as she straightened where the knife had come from. There was the ghost of a sheath, but even so it looked extremely dangerous.

Jala stood still for some time, and when she moved she was Jala again. She stepped indifferently over Telemann, not looking at him, over the body and over the blood; she walked magnificently to the door, opening it. She had heard the shouting and Comingo voices; she wasn't in any doubt. 'Father,' she called, 'Fa . . . ather.'

Mr Martin's answering shout came clearly.

'You can come in now. David has arranged it all.'

Major Gage and Mr Martin arrived together. David was standing by the table, and, not thinking, he picked the second slip of paper from Telemann's black hat. He read it idly, once and a second time. It said 'rifle and bayonet'.

He looked at Telemann, and Telemann was still smiling.

Chapter 13

Lord Brasted was standing outside the aircraft. It was three in the morning, and he wore pyjamas and a formidable dressing gown. A manservant was behind him with travelling rugs. He greeted Edward Carr urbanely, though he had been kept waiting. The hours preceding had, for both men, been very full ones. 'I'm delighted you could come,' Brasted said.

'I'm extremely sorry to have delayed you. The telegrams kept arriving, as I expect they did to you. There were a dozen things . . .'

'Of course there were. You must tell me about them. Not now, though.' Lord Brasted followed the Secretary of State into the aircraft. 'Not now, though.' He adjusted his seat, settling himself under the rugs. 'I am sixty,' he explained, 'and a little more. My health is excellent. But I sleep when I am sleepy. At the risk of apparent discourtesy sometimes – but I sleep.' He turned to the manservant. 'At nine o'clock, please.'

Edward Carr took another seat and a drink from the steward. He finished the whisky and glanced at Lord Brasted. Unmistakably Brasted was asleep.

At the Colony's brash airport Lord Brasted descended, but only for long enough to change. He walked to the knot of men which awaited him, the Associate amongst them but not Carey. He was affable but decided. 'You must excuse me for today,' he said. 'But tomorrow evening, of course, I shall hope to see you at the Firehouse.' The Firehouse was the

Company's grandest bungalow, something kept for visitors of status quite exceptional. He turned to the Associate. 'Will you see to the drinks, please?' Lord Brasted thought well of the Associate or he wouldn't have trusted him with drinks. The Associate was intelligent; trouble he shot superbly. But he wasn't quite what was wanted for St Cree's. 'Something to drink,' Brasted repeated.

'Of course, sir.'

With his servant Lord Brasted disappeared into a waiting-room.

He emerged in twenty minutes, immense and immaculate. A linen suit, magnificently tailored, swung from his still splendid shoulders. He was smoking a cheroot. In the tropical sunlight his eyeglass winked like a helio. On his head was a white topee and, incredibly, a brass spike crowned it. Lord Brasted caught the eye of Edward Carr and grinned; he tapped the topee affectionately. 'You can't just buy these nowadays,' he explained. 'I have to have them made.'

'It looks magnificent.'

The Minister hid a smile, for he was thinking that the topee was part of the act. It was a good act, too. People mostly liked it that Lord Brasted was Lord Brasted, and those who didn't, or those who were deceived . . . Edward Carr shrugged philosophically. In a moment or two, as soon as they were alone, Brasted would be serious. The Minister didn't doubt he would have everything in hand.

They walked to one of the two helicopters which were waiting. Lord Brasted shook hands with the pilot, turning to see that his servant and a secretary were safely in the other. The two machines rose smoothly, and almost at once the Colony's coastline was behind them. St Cree's was just visible, low in the horizon's haze. The island was visible, but not to Lord Brasted. Unabashed, he was asleep again.

They grounded on the harbour's little beach, and now the men awaiting them were fewer. There were David's two assistants, the Magistrate and, behind them, a leathery man in a hat too large for him. Brasted, astonishingly agile, jumped from the helicopter. 'You had my message?' he asked at once.

'We did, sir.'

'And sent Carr home – to the Valley.'

'Yes, sir.'

'Excellent. He has earned a holiday. But I have to talk to him, and urgently. We can go there now.'

'There are jeeps, of course. But it's pretty rough.'

But Lord Brasted wasn't listening; he had turned to the other man. 'Why, Monty,' he said.

'Why, Lord Brasted.'

'Who's he? . . . You got it out, I see.'

'Sure I got it out.'

'Lucky you were in the Colony.'

'I was close all right.'

'What's it worth?'

'To you?' The man in the hat shrugged. 'It's big,' he said. 'Anything up to seventy thousand, I should guess. And more to come.'

'I meant to you.'

'I wouldn't rob a friend. It didn't go too badly. I got it out in nine hours – while you were flying about. Say the usual. Say fifty grand.'

'Say twenty.'

'Forty.'

'Thirty.'

'Done.'

The man in the hat waved acceptance, and Lord Brasted turned to the jeeps as they bumped to a stop in the sand. 'We shan't need the other,' he told the assistant. He climbed into one with Edward Carr, and the driver let in the clutch.

They were skirting the airstrip when Lord Brasted removed his topee. The gesture wasn't calculated, but it was significant.

Brasted looked at Edward Carr, nodding towards the driver. 'Do you think he understands English?' he asked.

'A little, probably. Not our kind though, or not what matters.'

'We must risk it; we must talk. I'm sorry I had to sleep. Twenty years ago . . .'

'I was very glad to sleep myself.'

'Edward, I thank you.' Lord Brasted pointed at the wreckage of the Dakota. One of the engines, broken from its nacelle, was lying a hundred yards from what was left of the fuselage. It had an air of something more than physical detachment. 'Let us start on that,' Brasted said. 'Of the various aspects of this affair let us start on the political. That is for you, of course.'

'Indeed it is. It's one of the matters which delayed me at Blackbushe.'

'May I ask . . . ?'

'But certainly.' The Secretary of State lit a cigarette. 'It is extremely unfortunate,' he said levelly, 'that one of Clementi's aircraft should have crashed on this island. I shouldn't wonder if he didn't apologize.'

'But it is an awkward coincidence that it happened to be full of soldiers. Armed to the teeth.'

'Very awkward indeed – if anybody mentioned it. We ourselves shall not. We shall simply return the bodies.'

'I see,' Lord Brasted said slowly; he thought for a moment. 'You think you can get away with it?'

'*We* can. It's the sort of thing the Foreign Office does beautifully – about the only thing nowadays. And as for Clementi, what has he to gain by blowing the gaff? He hasn't got troops on to the island, and we have. Later he could start another tack, I suppose – start a major war: that's still open to him if he chooses, though my guess is still firmly that he doesn't. But for the moment he has failed. Why should he advertise his failure? Why should he uncover it?'

‘I see,’ Lord Brasted said again. But a thought struck him. ‘According to the messages we had before we left there were a dozen men here, paratroopers, before that aircraft crashed. They too are dead. And eight of them were shot. Not burnt, not unrecognizable. Just shot.’

‘Nobody,’ the Minister said blandly, ‘nobody looks in coffins. Unless they want to, that is. I am suggesting that emphatically Clementi does not.’

Lord Brasted chuckled. ‘You know your business,’ he said. ‘You’re a smoothie.’

It was a resounding compliment.

‘Thank you, James.’

Lord Brasted, now, he had begun to think aloud. ‘Very neat,’ he was saying, ‘very pretty. But a good many people know the truth besides Clementi.’

‘They do. But what sort of people? A few Kamblas, perhaps, whose story would be risky to run even if anybody knew that there was one to look for. Nobody’s getting a beat from the Kamblas. And Comingi – clansmen, men under discipline. Their headmen have told them to hold their tongues, and I haven’t any doubt of them. And finally one or two men of your own. I misjudge you, James, if they chatter against your wishes.’

‘You do not misjudge me. . . . And the officials?’

‘I can handle officials.’

‘I do not doubt it. But there were soldiers too – there was some shooting.’

‘There was some unavoidable shooting in the process of restoring order, and I shan’t attempt to hide it. Happily we had no casualties ourselves. Some men were killed – some men in what might have been a uniform. Or equally might not. There was nothing to identify it.’

‘It’s all very odd, though.’

‘I agree – it’s *very* odd. I’m not at all sure that we can soft pedal for ever, or not on everything. But for a little, I should hope. Politically that's all I ask. The island is ours still. And the oil. Tensions relax. What would be a sensation in May could be a border affray in June. With this oil decided . . .'

Lord Brasted nodded briefly.

The jeep had begun to climb the track into the hills. Brasted rode it surprisingly easily, rolling on his considerable nates. He considered the scenery, smiling, sniffing the mountain air. Presently he said: 'And Eeles?'

'Eeles has bought it.'

'Certainly he's bought it. The more we hear of this story, the more we consider his motives . . .'

'If you're thinking about that telegram, I propose to ignore it.'

'Do you think you can?'

'I don't see why not.' The Minister threw away his cigarette. 'My information,' he said formally, 'is that Sir Francis Eeles has had a nervous breakdown. I wouldn't be surprised if it were genuine, and if it isn't it's undeniably diplomatic. I shan't inquire and I shan't pursue. I don't feel irresponsible about that, I don't even feel cynical. A little outside the niceties perhaps.'

'Next item,' Lord Brasted said.

'Masters will be His Excellency.'

'Splendid.'

'That's all, I think. But I had one or two questions to ask you.'

'Naturally you had. The Company first, then. Carey has offered his resignation and I have accepted it. His attempt on Telemann I can forgive, and though to recall your brother at the crisis was ill-judged, I suppose there was a case for it. Of a sort. What is indefensible is that he should decline to accompany Eeles. That was – that was bad.'

'He'll have his pension,' Edward Carr said thoughtfully.

'And anything else you may care to throw in.'

'I'm afraid I don't follow you.'

'Commander would be too much, no doubt, but Officer. . . .'

'No,' the Minister said promptly.

'Perhaps you're right. He's a failure, of course; one doesn't want to rub it in.' Lord Brasted puffed for a while reflectively 'Then I was going to ask you about Telemann,' he said. 'Had you any plans?'

'I hadn't thought. I suppose we should have sent him back to Laramonda with the others.'

'No . . . I would prefer not. Would you do me a kindness and leave Telemann to me?'

'I can't see why not. He wasn't a Laramondan.'

'Indeed he was not.' Lord Brasted reached beneath his seat, producing a bag, drawing from it a considerable volume. '*de Gotha*,' he explained, 'the *Almanac*.' He opened at a page already marked and began to read. The recital, on Telemann's own lips, had taken some time: on Brasted's, sturdily mispronouncing, it seemed interminable. But it finished at last. 'Quite a man,' Brasted said.

'Quite a man.'

'Seven hundred years – it's a very long time.'

'Too long perhaps.'

'Perhaps. He was the last, it seems.' Lord Brasted looked again at the increasing greenery. 'All things must end,' he said almost to himself, 'and this shall end decently. In order. I will bury this man, if I may. We will put him in the chapel. A Christian he was born and a Christian he shall die. I'm a Calvinist myself, so death is important. We'll have a proper tomb. His arms . . .'

'His arms?'

'I can get them. He would like that, I think.'

Edward Carr did not answer, and Brasted was silent for some time. 'We must be nearly there,' he suggested.

'I should think so.'

'Your sister-in-law . . .'

'I'm frightened too.'

'Frightened? Too? But you misunderstand me. I simply can't wait. She sounds charming. It sounds quite perfect.'

'Not that again,' Edward Carr said dryly.

'Brasted on love, you mean? Well, perhaps not in detail. But I must insist that I'm delighted.'

'But I am not. That other girl, Margaret Harrison . . .'

'What was she like?'

'Intelligent and not bad-looking. Competent. A little money.'

'A match, in fact. As you once told me. Brasted should have approved but didn't. Brasted was an old fool.'

'Brasted is sometimes a little difficult to follow.'

Lord Brasted shook his head. 'Intelligent, not bad-looking, competent, and a little money,' he repeated. 'Quite fatal,' he announced decidedly. 'Not what I wanted for David at all.'

'Did you want a Cominga?'

'Of good education and excellent family? By all accounts a raving beauty? Why not?'

'We shall see,' Edward Carr said slowly.

The jeep bumped on the last of the track, through the wood in its cradling cliffs, into the open valley. Mr Martin met them at its mouth. He did it beautifully, a gentleman on his own ground. Lord Brasted stole a glance at Edward Carr. He was evidently impressed.

They walked to the little house and David presented Jala. His brother shook hands with her, but Brasted kissed her hand. It was something he did well; he didn't take her hand and raise it: he put his own beneath it, leaving the raising to her. 'Enchanted,' he said. 'Enchanting.' He looked at David. 'You are fortunate,' he told him.

Jala slipped away, returning with wine.

They drank with ceremony and Lord Brasted turned again to David and to Jala; he had prepared a little speech and he was going to shoot it. 'I have a house in London,' he began, 'which at the moment I do not need. I am taking my wife abroad, but there will be servants still.' Lord Brasted never said staff when he meant servants. He looked at Jala. 'I was hoping,' he went on, 'that you would make use of it.'

Jala glanced at David, for she had been thinking. Not now, she had decided, not England just yet. Later, of course, when the children . . .

'I'm not sure I want to go home,' David said slowly.

'But you quite misunderstand me. I hadn't the least intention of asking you to go home: on the contrary there is work for you here. I *want* you here; I want you to take Carey's place. I don't believe in single wells. This island floats on oil – I smell it. And if it doesn't you can drill off-shore. St Cree's can be another Maracaibo.' Lord Brasted waved his hand. 'There's work for years. You needn't move to the Colony unless you want to. Here is what matters. Live here and, if you have to, commute. I wouldn't blame you.'

'You're very kind.'

'I'm an excellent business man.'

'You didn't sack Carey, did you?'

'To be honest I didn't have to. He had only a year to go in any case. We'll concede him that for his pension.'

David took Jala's hand. 'Well?' he asked her.

'Stay, David. Wait a little.'

'I've always wanted to stay,' David said. 'In a way.'

'And the other way?' Brasted asked.

David drew a breath and, very slowly, exhaled it. 'There isn't another way,' he said. 'Not now.'

'Good. Excellent.' Lord Brasted's manner conveyed that he was pleased with himself. 'May I smoke?' he inquired. He produced his cheroot case, offering it to Mr Martin.

Mr Martin inspected the cheroots with a courteous suspicion. 'No thank you,' he said politely. But he was entirely firm.

In the opinion of Edward Carr he rose, and instantly, another notch.

Lord Brasted lit his cheroot. 'I was saying,' he went on, that you had misunderstood me. I was proposing no more than a visit – a honeymoon in fact.' His eyeglass flashed mischievously. 'I gather that the occasion had been somewhat curtailed.'

'You are very kind,' Jala said suddenly. She had been thinking again, and London, the splendid house which this splendid man must have ... David and London and David again. Unthinkable to hesitate.

Besides it would be very good practice.

'It is extremely kind of you,' she said again. 'We accept with great pleasure.'

'Good once more. Then that is settled. For six weeks, shall we say?'

'If so long is indeed convenient.'

Lord Brasted did not blink. 'Certainly it is.' He turned to Mr Martin. 'I should have explained that your son-in-law would have been obliged to come to England for a week or two in any case. I don't know whether he thought it worth while to mention that when he was last in London an attempt was made to murder him. Probably he didn't, but there was. He will have to appear at the trial, and that has been arranged.' Lord Brasted cocked an eye at the Secretary of State. 'I hope you don't mind,' he added. 'I thought it might save you embarrassment if the – er, the inquiries came from myself.'

'Not at all.'

'The matter has been adjusted. I remember suggesting that the police might learn a good deal from the affair, and they have. It seems that there are several people. . . . But none is within the jurisdiction but the two before the Court. Who have reasons of their own for silence in public. They will be tried for attempted murder, and if it is necessary to mention motive the suggestion will be robbery. The affair will be handled with tact and discretion: political overtones will be notably absent.' Lord Brasted glanced at the Minister again. 'That suits you, Edward?' he asked. 'That marches, I think, with your policy for this matter as a whole? *Quieta non movere. . . .*'

'Precisely.'

Lord Brasted returned to Mr Martin. 'I need not insist,' he told him, 'that the judiciary is entirely independent of the executive. I state the theoretical position. Naturally it is the grossest libel on the competence of the executive.'

Mr Martin nodded sagely. He hadn't understood all this and he suspected what, if he had known the word, he would have called a paradox. But he hadn't been deceived. This airy nobleman, a little talkative – he hadn't been born yesterday. 'Quite,' Mr Martin said wisely. 'Quite so.'

Edward Carr and Lord Brasted made their adieux. Brasted kissed Jala's hand again, murmuring over it something which made her blush and laugh. She was thinking that Lord Brasted was an old goat. She was a woman and sensible, and she hadn't any objection to old goats, particularly when they were so charming as Lord Brasted. She hadn't any objection, but it was to David she turned.

Edward Carr and Lord Brasted walked from the little house towards the jeep. Brasted was humming unmelodiously; he was in tearing form. 'Well?' he inquired. 'Well?'

Edward Carr was silent till they reached the jeep. 'I think it will do,' he said finally. He smiled a little wryly. 'I think you win,' he added.

'I try to,' Lord Brasted said happily.

More About Penguins

If you have enjoyed reading this book you may wish to know that *Penguin Book News* appears every month. It is an attractively illustrated magazine containing a complete list of books published by Penguins and still in print, together with details of the month's new books. A specimen copy will be sent free on request.

Penguin Book News is obtainable from most bookshops; but you may prefer to become a regular subscriber at 3s for twelve issues. Just write to Dept. EP, Penguin Books Ltd., Harmondsworth, Middlesex, enclosing a cheque or postal order, and you will be put on the mailing list.

Some other books published by Penguins are described on the following pages.

Note: *Penguin Book News* is not available in the U.S.A.

The Case of the Perjured Parrot

Erle Stanley Gardner

Sabin's pet parrot, Casanova, was left by the murderer in the mountain cabin beside the corpse, and eleven days later the bird raised the alarm. Sabin's son enlists Perry Mason's help in the solution of the mystery, involving a breakneck visit to the mountains, interviews with the sheriff, a marriage of doubtful legality, a librarian's love affair, and a surprising inquest. The story moves at rattling speed to the satisfactory ending.

Another Penguin by William Haggard

Venetian Blind

Information on Negative Gravity was leaking to a foreign power; and Negative Gravity was central to the nation's defence.
Richard Wakeley, pitched raw into an issue of national jeopardy, watches a big industrialist and his Venetian stepdaughter play out their ambiguous parts.

The puzzles of a 'who-dunnit?' generate the smouldering tensions of a 'who'll-do-it?' in this characteristic thriller by the author who has been called 'The adults' Ian Fleming'.

Also by William Haggard

Slow Burner

'The atmosphere of high-grade scientific, civil, and secret services is convincing. Thoroughly recommendable' – *Observer*

Slow Burner was the first spy-thriller by a writer who has managed, in one successful novel after another, to fuse the excitement of Ian Fleming with C. P. Snow's acute knowledge of the Whitehall country. Here he introduces that suave, likeable Security chief, Colonel Charles Russell. A vital atomic secret has leaked out. Russell prefers to play fair, but, surrounded by intrigue and treachery, he knows very well how to play rough too.